Trust In Love

Persimmon Hollow Legacy
Novella 1

Gerri Bauer

D1367004

E-pub ISBN: 978-1-7328711-0-6
Print ISBN: 978-1-7328711-1-3

Cover art by SelfPubBookCovers.com/RLSather

*To my husband, Peter D. Bauer, for his love
and support.*

Chapter 1

Persimmon Hollow, Florida
December 1891

Margaret's wrist trembled from the weight of the serving tray balanced on her shoulder and upturned fingertips. She overcompensated to alleviate the pressure, causing the tray to tilt. Stoneware clattered on the dry-sink counter.

She steadied the cutlery and crocks before anything else crashed. "Saints in heaven, please don't let another thing break," she muttered. The cook scowled at her from across the kitchen. "That'll be coming out of your paycheck, for sure." Tired eyes stared out of her doughy face. "Don't say I didn't warn ya."

Don't I know it, thought Margaret. She'd already broken a soup bowl and glass pitcher earlier in the week. Now something else would go on her demerit list. Soon she'd be owing money to the Persimmon Hollow Railroad Hotel instead of the other way around. She had worked as a maid and nanny since she was fifteen and had never in those ten years felt so inept as she did at this hotel service.

As she squatted to get the tray level with the counter and slide the laden platter onto its surface, her body rebelled. She grappled to hold back the sliding stoneware and the tray finally steadied.

"'Tis a miracle, for sure and for certain," she said.

"No, just me," came a voice behind her. Margaret gave a start, but instinct, trained by wariness, rooted her in place. She kept her hands glued on the tray. "Who?" She glanced over her shoulder, wide-eyed, straight into the gaze of a grinning Francesco Bartolomeo, who stood inches behind her with one hand steading the tray on her shoulder. The Francesco Bartolomeo. She blinked, willed her heart to stop its ridiculous rush of beats, and aimed to wrestle command of the situation.

"Thank you," she said, with a slight tilt of her head. She knew she looked a fright, her hair frizzing in the Florida humidity and her clothes clinging to her clammy skin, but nothing could be done for it. They were too far inland for a sea breeze to stir the air.

"There, on the end, there's some room." He pushed back a jumble of dirty plates, mugs, pitchers, and bowls with a muscled arm, then lifted the tray and set it down. "It's not fit for you to carry such weight."

"Many thanks, but I can manage," Margaret said. She ignored the welcome release in her shoulder and wrist muscles, and concentrated instead on yet another barb to her inadequacy at the hateful job. "I'm up to the task." She transferred dishes from tray to counter.

Francesco stepped back as she edged him aside. "Absolutely. Of course you are. I meant no disrespect."

She glanced up, searching for a spark of sarcasm, but saw sincerity in his gaze. A hint of perplexity, even. Margaret frowned but managed another nod and focused on the job at hand. Unload the dishes. Carefully. Without breaking anything else. Go back to the dining room and wait on a table. Repeat. Thank the Lord for sending this most able and agreeable assistance in this most strange and inhospitable job in an unfamiliar land.

As she covertly eyed him, she bit back the smile that threatened to rise. She could hardly believe that the handsomest man on the premises was helping her. No, make that the most dangerous man on the premises. Even she, outsider on the staff that she was, had been warned about his overly friendly ways.

Yet, that was just it. He was being friendly. Nothing more. She sensed no leering, no forwardness, none of the preening and pushiness she'd seen among men of questionable character. None of the attitude she'd encountered in— She stopped herself. She wouldn't think about the past. She pushed aside memories of the incidents that had precipitated her detour to this backwater, a place so raw some buildings still smelled of sawdust.

Persimmon Hollow was growing, or so she was told. Downtown was expanding beyond its four-block, wooden-sidewalk main thoroughfare. The academy just north of downtown was almost finished constructing an additional building, for study of science and music, she'd heard. Citrus groves wrapped around homesteads and hotels. For such a small town, Persimmon Hollow had five hotels. She worked at the most impressive one. Still, Florida was a frontier compared to the city streets she'd known since arriving in America.

Maybe the men in Florida were different than up north. No, that would be silly. A man was a man. She wished she weren't so aware of this one, but she knew all about him and his work. The other waitresses loved to gossip about him.

Her gaze strayed to his hands as he quietly resumed helping her clear the tray. Strong and clean. Some nicks and scrapes and calluses, to be expected when one blacksmithed and drove wagons, she supposed.

The kitchen door banged open. "Miss Margaret Murphy, where are you? Your tables are waiting!" Mrs. Pendleton's voice rang out.

"Ah, sounds like you better go," Francesco said.

"Indeed," said Margaret, again not sure if he were being sarcastic or not. "Mrs. P has little patience with me." She wiped her hands on her apron and reached to shake his hand. "I do thank you." *Keep things nice and impersonal, Margaret.*

"At your service." Francesco gave a slight bow. A thick lock of his dark hair dropped over his forehead as he straightened. "Glad I showed up at just the right time." He glanced at her outstretched hand and then to her eyes, and then away.

Oh, he's good, she thought. Advance and retreat. The others were right to warn about him. She drew back her hand and busied it with smoothing her apron.

"Miss Murphy!"

For once she was pleased to hear Mrs. P's demanding voice. "Coming!" she said, and hurried off without saying goodbye to Francesco.

- - -

Margaret hurried across the room, careful to not let the heels of her shoes clatter on the wooden floor. She met her coworker Hortense under a wide window that gave the diners a view of the hotel grounds. Her eyes were drawn to the cedar and pine trees that edged a winding walkway that led to the main road. The view was nice, but they all would have fared better with cooler temperatures.

Hortense had her back to the window, instead concentrating on the crowded room. "You think they'd have added more help when they doubled the size of the dining room."

Margaret plunked down her empty tray on the serving station the two shared. Around her she heard the murmur of dinner talk and the clink of cutlery on ceramicware.

"But no," continued Hortense, "I heard the cook even has to fill in as dishwasher today. Can you believe it? The dishwasher went home sick. Let's hope he gets well or finds some friend or relative to take the spot, or it might be one of us back there, arms in dirty dishwater up to our elbows."

"Wouldn't be the first time for me," Margaret said and pitched in to help after checking the needs of her assigned tables. She had four more to clear after the diners left, plus the big one in the back where the patrons appeared in no hurry to move. There'd be no time for crochet work tonight. Again.

"Dishwashing is not my job," Hortense said. "Or yours. Oh, look!" Hortense glanced out one of the side windows as she moved away from the workstation. "There goes that Francesco. Looks like he came out the kitchen door. Did you see him in there?"

Margaret resisted answering. She wasn't usually welcomed into the embrace of chatter about the blacksmith-driver. She wasn't an outcast, she just wasn't included. Why give Hortense anything she and the others would dissect later?

"You did, didn't you?" Hortense declared. "You're not answering, you must have. Gosh. Listen to what I warned you: be careful around that one. You're still new here. You don't know. He's a ladies' man for sure, the way he looks at everyone with those blue eyes and makes everyone think they're his special friend. Who knows what else he wants. You can't tell with these foreigners. On top of that, I heard he's Catholic. Oh, sorry, Margaret, I didn't mean anything bad. I know you live at that orphanage run by the religious ladies on the next property. It's just..." Her voice trailed.

Margaret was relieved to hear the clink of silverware tapped against a glass. One of the diners at the back table signaled to her. She hurried over, hoping the housekeeper hadn't noticed that a patron had to call for service, but mostly glad to end the conversation with Hortense. She'd felt the sting of Hortense's words. She wondered whether staff members gossiped about her, also a foreigner and a Catholic, when she wasn't around.

Hortense was friendlier than others on the staff. But they were worlds apart in many ways. Margaret was on unfamiliar ground, new to the town, so small after her city life, and new to the job. And clumsy at it. She wasn't accustomed to the fast pace of the hotel and the worldliness of the people who visited and worked there. Best to stay on her guard.

Chapter 2

Hours later, Margaret shed her wrinkled uniform, which was sticky with humidity and sweat. In two swift motions, she pulled a dressing gown over her head and released her light auburn hair from the tight bun, letting it frizz around her face. No one in this tropical zone stayed fresh. She was having a hard time even remembering they were still in the Christmas holiday season.

She sank into a chair, heaved a sigh, and kicked at the water in the foot basin as she told her cousin Bridget about her day. "And then, Mrs. P, she's the housekeeper, gave me a dressing down at the meeting of all the workers after supper, and reminded me I now have three broken items to pay for."

Bridget tied a knot in a strand of thread at the end of her needle, and picked up her mending. "I'm beginning to regret recommending the job and encouraging you to move here."

"It gets worse," Margaret said. "After the meeting, Mrs. P pulled me aside and said if I didn't improve she'd be forced to let me go."

Margaret stretched each one of her toes individually in the water she'd scented with sprigs of lavender and lemon balm. She had to admit, it was nice that pretty things grew year-round in this land of sunny warmth.

"Oh, no, Bridget, I don't regret coming. You're a lifesaver. I'm grateful you arranged the job. It's not your fault I'm clumsy at it. Who would of thought waitressing was so difficult? It always looked easy at the homes I worked in up north. Plus, everybody at the hotel is exhausted. The housekeeper can be nice, but she's so overworked she's short-tempered most all the time."

"Still, I'm starting to question whether either of us made the right decision."

"Bridget, you know how much I need this job."

"Aye."

"Every penny I can send back home is a help." She thought of her family and how the coins helped keep starvation at bay and a roof over their heads, and eased her conscience for causing part of the problem in the first place.

"I guess nobody in this town needs Irish crochet lace or its maker." Margaret didn't even phrase her inquiry as a question. No one, it seemed, had use for her handicraft unless she were giving it away. How could she have been such a fool? Swindled! She winced at the memory and blew out a breath. So many mistakes.

Bridget looked up and met her gaze with compassion. "No, there's no market right now for commissions, I'm afraid. Persimmon Hollow is growing, but we're still a small settlement. Once you make a collection of items, perhaps we can appeal to shopkeepers to carry the pieces."

Margaret snorted and looked at the clock on the mantel. She'd barely get enough sleep before having to return to the hotel for breakfast duty. If she managed to knot together a few rows of yarn before nodding off, she'd consider it a good night. At such a rate, she might finish a collar and cuff set in a couple of weeks. One set.

And that was only after she devoted some of her precious free minutes to teaching her craft to the children. It was how she repaid Bridget and the other sisters for letting her board with them at St. Isidore Orphanage.

"You never know what God will bring us," Bridget said. "Have faith, Margaret." She continued to mend a patch in boy-sized trousers with slow, smooth stitches.

"I forgot to tell you, I asked if I could have off for Mass next Sunday," Margaret said after a bit. "Father is coming to town that day, right?"

"Yes, praise God, we're to have Mass here on Epiphany Sunday," Bridget said. "Someday our parish will be large enough for a priest to be assigned full time. Bless them all, who work so hard to bring the sacraments to those of us in missionary territories."

"The housekeeper said she doubted I could go," Margaret said. The hotel was certainly not missionary territory. One of the first things she noticed had been the wealth and leisure of the people who frequented the place, compared to her own background and to the Catholic community and many other residents in Persimmon Hollow, at least what she'd seen of them.

"The guests come first, the housekeeper keeps reminding me, and some guests may wish an early breakfast," Margaret continued. "I have to be there to serve because guests expect to see the same face during their stay. 'Like family,' said the housekeeper. Right, some family."

Bridget set down her mending. This time, her glance was troubled. "They can't refuse you leave for worship, can they?"

"They can."

"The outside of that hotel is so grand, it's hard to imagine people inside might struggle to do the right thing," Bridget said.

"Their idea of right is different than yours or mine," Margaret said. She wondered if being a religious sister meant one had to assume every person on the planet was good at heart. Bridget certainly thought so.

"I'm just glad I get to stay here with you instead of living with the other servants," Margaret said, to change the subject. "They sleep all the way on the top half-floor of the hotel. There's no air up there. I can hardly breathe up there when I go to freshen up between morning and noon mealtimes." She didn't add that not everyone was as welcoming to her as Hortense was.

Margaret started to dry her sore feet on a cotton towel. In six hours, she'd have to get up, dress, walk down the sandy road, cross the railroad tracks, traipse up the long, wide drive to the hotel, and repeat this day all over again. And do the same the next day. And the next.

Margaret closed her eyes to recollect herself. In the bleakness behind her lids, she thought of Francesco and his friendly smile. Was Hortense right? Or might she instead find a fellow friend who understood her outsider feelings? He, too, was forced to work closely with longtime Americans. Surely she wasn't the only one who found them so hard to figure out.

- - -

"Miss Murphy, you simply must understand I cannot allow you to start work late next Sunday," the housekeeper said during distribution of wages the next afternoon.

Margaret opened her mouth to protest but the housekeeper held up a hand. "Your church service is at seven-thirty a.m., you say, in the middle of town proper. That's two miles distant. It will be after nine o'clock before you arrive back here, at the earliest. You have duties here. We have arranged for a preacher among the guests to say a few words at Bible-reading between meals. That will have to suffice."

Margaret shook her head. "It's not the same. It's not a Mass."

The housekeeper peered at her over the top of her glasses, not unkindly, and clucked. "I'm sorry, dear."

She picked up Margaret's pay envelope from the pile on her desk, frowned, and tapped a finger on it. "Right now, your attention should be on better handling of the dishware. I regret we had to deduct for three pieces this week. Let's focus on proper serving, shall we? The New Year's Eve celebration is almost here and it must go off without mishap."

The housekeeper looked beyond Margaret's shoulder while handing her the pay envelope. "Next!" she called.

Dismissed, Margaret stepped aside so the person behind her could receive their meager allotment of cash. She pressed her lips together to bite back a retort as she exited the housekeeper's office.

She slipped around the hall corner to avoid the prying eyes of others in line, and opened her pay envelope. And gasped in silent shock.

How much could three broken pieces of stoneware cost? She counted the money again, to be sure she hadn't missed a stray coin or bill. Nope. Her face stung as though slapped. She wanted to hurl the envelope and shout out her anger. Instead, she forced calm steps upon her feet. Head high, she aimed for the doors, eager to reach the outdoors and escape the stifled hush of what felt like forced servitude.

Margaret stood on the back steps. No manicured grounds here. Servants were allowed to take air in the work area behind the kitchen and hall of offices. A cluster of three pine trees behind the smokehouse provided some shade and hint of seclusion to an area that was otherwise all business.

She often went back to the orphanage between lunch and dinner service. Not today. No way did she want to see Bridget's expected calm acceptance of her pitiful pay, likely delivered with counsel to aim for improvement. I'm doing the best I can, Bridget, she yelled in her head, and stalked toward the pines.

Margaret plopped down on a bed of pine straw and stewed. She pulled out the rosary she kept tucked inside her skirt pocket, then shoved it back in. She wouldn't plead to the Blessed Mother with angry prayers.

At least the day wasn't so hot. A gentle breeze caressed her. Margaret leaned her head back against a tree trunk and closed her eyes. The slight, dry wind made her ache for the misty rains and cool embrace of her homeland and its gentle seasons. Her whole time in America, until now, had been in a city with clear-cut winter and summer. The changing seasons had helped her grow accustomed to a place that was a crowded mess of folks one atop the other. Now she'd gone clear beyond anything familiar. She struggled to accept the summerlike winter in Persimmon Hollow, the place's strange greenery, and its squeaky newness.

She blinked her eyes open at the sound of leaves rustling nearby. A new shadow fell over her.

Francesco stood there, hands in his pockets of his farrier apron.

"Okay for me to join you?"

She sensed a hesitancy in him that belied the gossip. "Why not," she said. "Not my trees."

"I'm not sure that's a welcome, but I'll take it." He sat down next to her.

Margaret glanced at the foot or so between them. Francesco shifted and put more distance between them. She steeled herself. Then exhaled. This fellow wasn't her former employer, the man who started what became her downward spiral to Florida. Francesco wasn't trying to swindle her, like the pretend beau who'd squandered her money and trust. Francesco didn't have any power over her or her future. They were equals, sort of.

Still, she vowed to keep her reserve in place.

"I saw you rush out of the hotel," Francesco said. "Everything all right?"

That's right; start with concern. Margaret hated being cynical but she'd learned her lesson. She didn't answer him.

"I can tell when something's wrong with a woman," he prodded. "I have four sisters."

"Four? Your family might be as large as mine." Whoa. Stop. Don't fall for the trap of familiarity. Her former beau had tried exactly that approach, and it had worked. "Why do you care what's wrong with me?" She met Francesco's gaze fully. "It's not like we're friends. You don't even know me, or I you."

"I wish to get to know you better," he said. "As for my family, I have two brothers too. There are seven of us, nine with my parents. Not too much for an Italian family." He lifted his shoulders in a half-shrug and gave her an equally half-smile that carried more than a hint of likeability. "I miss my family a lot. You?"

She was confounded. Was he playing around, or genuinely nice and trying to find common ground? Margaret was tired, ornery, and in no mood for games.

"Why me, and why now? You know, everyone talks about you like you are some kind of...um...some kind of Lothario, so pardon my prickliness."

Hortense and the other women on staff were full of chatter about Francesco. Margaret knew that, as farrier and buggy driver, he fashioned ironwork and carted patrons to and from the train depot and on excursions to freshwater springs, citrus groves, the St. Johns River, and even as far as the Atlantic Ocean. He had a reputation of being able to charm even the grumpiest hotel patron, not to mention his fellow workers.

She glanced over his face, hair, and natural athletic build. She noticed all far too quickly when he sat down.

"Uh, Lothario?" he asked. "I haven't heard that word yet in my studies of English."

Well, she hadn't either. It was Hortense's word, and she'd been too embarrassed to betray her own ignorance.

She shrugged. "It's what the other workers say."

"But what does it mean?" he persisted.

She puffed out a breath. "Who knows what these Americans mean half the time? Maybe it's a word they know from up north. They all come down here for winter and then go to New England to work at the railroad's hotels for summer and they think that makes them special. They all have more school learning than I do. They come from families that have been American forever. What do I know? I'm the odd one, the only foreign girl among them."

"We're outsiders together," Francesco said. "I won't go north with the others after the hotel closes for summer, either. My job in the off-season, that's what they call it, is to be caretaker of both the property and the animals."

He paused for a minute. "I think it's because they got me … how do you say in American … they got me cheap. Two for one, building and animals."

Margaret snorted a half-laugh. "Not as cheap as they're getting me." She waved her pay envelope. "I lost more than half my pay this week to cover the cost of dishes I broke. At this rate, I'll soon owe them more than I earn."

He frowned. "You're a hard worker. I'm surprised."

She flicked a glance at him. Had he been watching her? Why? She knew she was attractive, but she was far from the prettiest girl around. She certainly was the clumsiest. Did he take her for easy prey, the way her former beau had?

"Why are you glaring at me?" Francesco asked.

"Because I don't know why you're being so friendly."

"I'm friendly to everybody," he protested. "It's the best way to get to be American, right? That's how Americans are—good-natured, pat on the back. This is easy for me. Back home, I know everybody and everybody knows me. I try to be the same here. You're newer here at the hotel than I am. So I say hello, make you feel welcome."

He looked up at a hawk perched high in one of the pine trees. "Other parts of being American, they're not so easy for me, though. I try to be my friendly self when I have to go into town. Some people there aren't as glad to see me as the tourists are when they get off the train and I'm there to help with baggage."

Margaret's thoughts veered between scoffing at him and believing him. He was really good at his game, or he was telling the truth. Either way, she had no intention of falling into a trap of caring what happened to him in town.

"I heard the accent still in your voice," Francesco said, after Margaret didn't respond to his explanation. "Not heavy, like in mine, but enough for me to notice."

Margaret stood up. His innocent comment struck a nerve she'd been trying to ignore.

"Yes, I'm a foreigner, different than the other girls. You're right. I'm not like them. I can't talk about how this ancestor or that has lived in some town or other for a hundred years. I'm not Protestant like they are. I'm probably the only Catholic on the entire staff."

"That makes two of us." Francesco scrambled up to stand next to her.

She felt better, knowing he understood and shared the faith that was so important to her. She cautiously lowered her reserve the smallest bit. He wasn't the man who'd wronged her, she reminded herself.

"I hope you and I can be friends, that I can learn from you something more about how to act American when I go away from the hotel," Francesco said. "In return, I can maybe help you be more happy on the job? You work so hard, but you sometimes look almost angry, not smiling or anything."

He shrugged. "I can tell you've been in the United States longer than me just by the way you talk. Your accent isn't as strong as mine. I figured you know a lot more about American ways than I do."

"I'm learning the hard way, as you can see." She held out her hand with the now-crumpled pay envelope in it. "I don't wish my methods on anyone."

A bit of the light went out of Francesco's eyes. "I see I have intruded." He bowed to her. "I apologize. Forget that I asked anything."

"No, it's all right." She owed him more than the judgment she'd offered. He didn't know why she had been defensive. He'd extended a hand of friendship, and she'd slapped it away for no reason.

"It's hard for me to make friends here," she said. They faced each other now, and she noticed his head-taller stature. "I guess I don't have to explain how it feels to not always understand the jokes or the reasons for acting a certain way or working a certain way. The others are nice enough to my face, but they keep their distance. I keep my head down and work. I don't have that gift of openness you have."

She neglected to say she'd once had it. How her determination had once been fueled by optimism, not desperation.

Francesco nodded. "Even I sometimes have to work at it. The jokes—sometimes I laugh without knowing why. Other times, people—like the ones I saw at the livery stable—are cross with me just because I'm Italian." His voice lowered. "One man called me a 'wop' when I passed by him at the store entryway. I didn't even know what the word meant. One of the other fellows here explained. I don't understand why that man at the livery stable felt the need to insult me just because I'm from Italy."

"Ouch," Margaret said. "I've seen and heard my share of 'No Irish Need Apply' signs and comments. Some workers at the hotel may think it, even if they don't say it to my face. As for the guests, people like them are accustomed to having the Irish serve them."

She tried to keep bitterness out of her voice, but Francesco's glance conveyed understanding.

"So, friends?" he asked. He reached out as though to shake her hand. Margaret almost laughed. He was being so formal.

"Friends," she said and accepted the handshake. His hand felt strong, and her own fit snugly into it. Lightness coursed through her. Their outsider connection buoyed her.

Maybe he was a ladies' man, and maybe he wasn't. She'd protect her heart and embrace the unity of shared understandings. "Between the two of us, we might be able to figure out how Americans think and act," she said. "Decide what parts of their culture we want to adopt."

"And what parts not to," he added.

Shared laughter softened Margaret's pain at having almost no money to send home this week.

"Maybe you really can help me figure how to keep my job," she said, serious again. She hated to ask for help, but she needed it.

"Happy to." Francesco glanced at the angle of the sun. "Speaking of jobs, I have to go. It's almost time to feed the horses."

Margaret watched him lope away. Maybe the gossips were wrong.

Chapter 3

"Need some help?"

Margaret looked up from behind the mountain of silverware piled in front of her on the wood-slat service table in the outdoor work area.

"Well, sure, but don't you have anything to do?" She pushed the jar of polish and a clean rag toward Francesco.

"Not for a while." Francesco pulled a battered watch fob from a small pocket slit in his pant's waistband. "Train's due with new arrivals in two hours, so I have some time before I have to leave to go get them."

Margaret sighed. "One of the other waitresses was supposed to help me but she claimed she has a headache." She picked up another fork, frowned at the elaborate scrollwork on the handle, and applied a vigorous rub of her rag. "It's endless. I've been at it since right after breakfast. Do they really need all this for the New Year's Eve dinner? Honestly, it's a bigger deal than Christmas to these people."

"I don't get it either," Francesco said. "There wasn't even a Midnight Mass at Christmas. Nobody seemed to care. That's what I mean when I say I'm trying to learn the customs here. I watch how people act and what they do. I watch all the time because it's how I learn how to be American. Like you."

"I'm not American," she replied. "I'm Irish."

"You look American. I don't."

"That doesn't make it any easier. I've been here five years and it's still not easy. What about you?"

"Six months."

"Six months! That's all?"

"Yeah, I came right after I turned twenty-six, after my brothers got old enough to step into my role at home. You look surprised. Why?"

"Yes, I'm surprised. You speak English well. I mean, you have that accent but you don't sound like a lot of the Italians I heard up north."

"A priest tutored me and other village children from the time we were small," Francesco said. "He said we'd need to know English if we wanted a future in America. And where I'm from, America is second only to the Promised Land."

Francesco pulled a pile of spoons toward him and started to polish. "He worked hard for us, Father Russo did. He set up an English language school just for us. We weren't always as dedicated as he hoped, though."

Margaret stopped polishing and listened. She shook her hands to relieve the cramp and tension from gripping the silverware.

"Just before he died, he urged us to…What word did he use? Aspire, that's it," Francesco said. "He said we should aspire to more than we could get from the," Francesco pursed his lips and furrowed his brow, "feudal, yes, feudal way of life we had there. We had no chance to better ourselves."

Margaret's lips thinned into a half-grimace. "My family left Ireland because the landlord pushed the rent so high we couldn't afford to eat. We still don't have enough to eat here, either. That's why I'm at this job." *Except the family table would be laden with more than bone soup and bread but for my own stupidity.* "That's why I was so upset yesterday when my pay was so low."

Someone yelled "Fore" at the hotel's adjacent nine-hole golf course, behind the tall pines. A burst of masculine laughter followed.

"Someday, I'll be one of the people playing golf," Francesco said.

"If they let you on the golf course," Margaret couldn't help but add.

"I know it's hard, Margaret. I try not to get bitter. Listen, soon as I can, let me help you send a little more to your family. I also send money home, like you. As much as I can. Family is important." He looked up at a noise in a pine tree, where a squirrel jumped from one branch to another.

"I didn't tell you about my family and my pay to make you feel obliged," Margaret hastened to say.

"Not obliged, just being a friend. It can't happen soon anyway. I'll be paying my *padrone* for another six months."

"Your what?"

"The *padrone*. He's like a job broker who helped us come to the United States and get employment. He claims a big fee for the job and transport service. Takes a chunk of my pay each month."

"That's awful." Margaret slammed down a sparkling silver spoon.

"We had to use him to get here," Francesco said. "A lot of Italians do, and some have it a lot worse than me. Father Russo made sure we had signed contracts, me and three other fellows who left at the same time. He read every word before letting us sign. And because we could read and write, this particular *padrone* wasn't able to trick us the way they do so many others. I'm glad I'll be free from him in only six more months."

"What'll you do then?"

"Maybe stay here. I'd like to open a blacksmith shop, and this seems as good as anywhere. The weather reminds me of home. I have to make sure the townspeople will accept me first. What about you? Will you stay here?"

"I don't know." She didn't want to tell him how much she disliked her job and wasn't too keen on Persimmon Hollow. The weather certainly didn't remind her of home. It was bright and hot, not cool and welcoming. Florida was green, she'd give it that. Green everywhere. But hard, like the edges of the plant leaves called palmettos, not soft like so much of the Irish countryside.

She looked at Francesco, intent at scrubbing off tarnish from a curve in a spoon handle. Was he always so optimistic? Between him and Bridget, a person would think the world was a happy place all the time. Even when it wasn't.

"Right now I'm just trying to earn my way and do what I can for my family," she said.

"You have time to think about it," he said. "They keep the hotel open until April."

The back door scraped opened and slammed closed.

"Oh, here comes my helper, finally," Margaret said.

Francesco rose. A pouting Arabelle, whose last name Margaret couldn't remember, flopped down beside her. Francesco sat back down.

"Miraculous recovery?" Margaret asked.

Arabelle scowled at her. "You know very well Mrs. P ordered me out here. She makes us work no matter what. Polishing silverware shouldn't be my job anyway. My head aches so badly and this polish will make it worse. I'm not sure how long I'll last."

"That's why I'm here—to help you lovely ladies," Francesco said. "Send some more knives, forks, and spoons my way."

"At least it's a nice day," Margaret added, and realized Francesco's cheeriness had started to rub off on her.

"Oh, it's much too warm," Arabelle complained. She fluttered her eyes toward Francesco. "But thank you. You are so kind and gentlemanly to help poor little me."

An unwelcome surge of annoyance flooded Margaret. She polished harder. And noticed Arabelle had yet to pick up a utensil or cleaning rag.

"Always happy to help a pretty lady," Francesco said, and kept at his work.

Margaret almost dropped the fork she held. He hadn't called her pretty. No, he'd called her determined, unsmiling, and a hard worker. Her defenses rose.

"It's a happy day when I can help two pretty ladies," Francesco said, his cheer undiminished.

"I think the breeze is better on that side of the table," Arabelle announced. She stood up and relocated herself a mite too close to Francesco for Margaret's taste.

Margaret bristled, then chided herself. *Why do you care?*

Honestly, though, she realized she wanted to be the one sitting next to him. Instead, she sat behind a pile of unpolished cutlery while Arabelle tilted her head and smiled at Francesco, who smiled back in return.

Margaret could live in America for a hundred years and never be able to coo at a man, no matter how attracted to him she might be. It just wasn't in her nature.

She didn't want to be attracted to Francesco, but in her heart she knew she was.

Arabelle made a vapid attempt to polish a spoon.

"Here, that's not the best way to do it," Francesco said. "Let me show you."

"Oh, would you, please?" Arabelle simpered.

Margaret closed her eyes for a few seconds, so that envy didn't green their already emerald color.

"Thank you," Arabelle sighed after the lesson.

Margaret kept her head down and polished with even more vigor.

"Everything okay, Margaret?" Francesco asked after some minutes of silence.

For a man with four sisters, he could be obtuse, she decided. "No, everything's fine," she said, in as cheerful a voice as she could muster, with a fake smile plastered on her face.

Francesco looked relieved. "That's good." He checked his watch.

"Time for you to go?" Margaret asked. They were never going to get the silver finished before lunch service began. She started to bundle the pieces and place them in the silver chests to carry inside.

"Yes, my time here is over," he said.

"Oh, so soon?" Arabelle asked.

Her voice sounded so phony that Margaret and Francesco caught each other in a surprised glance of amusement. Francesco raised an eyebrow.

Margaret grinned.

- - -

That night, she saw Francesco again as she rounded the side of the hotel on her way home after a long dinner service. He helped the last guest off a barouche. Then, instead of getting back on, he gently started to lead the horses around and toward the direction of the stables.

She waved. His return wave indicated a wish that she come his way.

She detoured over to him.

"Just getting back?" she asked, somewhat surprised. The train station wasn't that far away.

"From a ride to look at the citrus groves," he said. "It's one of guests' favorite evening rides. It's a big deal for them to pick an orange or two right from a tree."

"That's a marvel to me too," she said. "Never saw anything like those trees."

"They remind me of home," Francesco said. For the first time since meeting him, Margaret saw a dimming of his habitual cheeriness.

"Nothing in Florida reminds me of Ireland," she said, and laughed at the idea of it. "But my family is much closer than yours, only a few days by train. I stay here with my cousin, so I don't have to live at the hotel."

"You're lucky," Francesco said. "I miss my family. A lot. My family and the ways of my village. Right now, Christmas season, we always have a procession to the church. It's a tradition that goes back so far nobody knows when it started. I can see the men carrying the statue of the Madonna, and the women carrying candles, and everybody singing. First the procession, then Mass, then a big feast."

He was quiet for a moment. "This is the first time in my life I'm not there for it."

Margaret reached and touched her hand to his, just for a moment, just enough to convey how much she understood.

"Thank you," he said.

They stood there, suddenly awkward in the soft dark. Francesco stared at the ground, then looked her in the face.

"Do you mind if I call on you sometime?" he blurted.

Margaret felt a little jolt inside. Her face flushed. "I'd...yes, I'd like that." So much for keeping her distance.

His eyes remained intent on hers. "I would, too."

The night wrapped around them. Piano music drifted out the open windows of the hotel's parlor area. A woman's voice tinkled above indistinguishable conversations in the distance, then quieted.

"I should be getting on," Margaret said. "Bye for now." She shifted her weight from one foot to the other. Not knowing how to leave with grace, she made an abrupt turn toward the sandy roadway that led away from the hotel.

Francesco touched her arm and she stopped. He took her hands and kissed them, then stepped back.

Margaret opened her mouth, closed it, stared, and then smiled. Francesco's charm returned in his grin.

"Good night, Miss Margaret," he said, and doffed his hat. "I regret only that I can't give you a ride home in this fancy vehicle, but the hotel's strict about the help not using it."

"My feet know the way," she said, ignoring the swelling from hours standing on them. She was conscious of her wrinkled uniform after a day's work, and of tangled tresses under her waitress cap.

"Until tomorrow, then," he said.

She waved a shy farewell and wandered off, full of lightness for the first time since arriving in Persimmon Hollow three weeks earlier.

When she was halfway home, Margaret realized she'd forgotten to give Francesco directions to where she lived.

Chapter 4

New Year's Eve, 1891

Anyone who could be on edge, was. Margaret stopped draping tables with clean linen and wiped her cheek with the edge of her apron. The midday meal had been long and the room overly warm, with cook in a grumpy mood because the dumplings had been heavy. The night's holiday banquet loomed like a burden, because of inadequate help, and guests were cranky because the unseasonably hot day had chased them from their midday constitutionals.

Margaret's hair, already prone to flyaway misbehavior, further rebelled in the humidity. Tendrils escaped every which way from the topknot under her cap.

"Neaten your tresses before tonight," Mrs. P barked after a half-glance at Margaret, then continued through the room on inspection. "Hurry with set up and preparations, everyone. I want all of you fresh and rested for tonight."

Margaret and Hortense exchanged glances at their shared service station. "I'm sure the half hour I might find to relax will do me a world of good," Margaret said. "Oh, wait, I'll need to spend it fixing my hair."

There would be no stopping at the orphanage for an afternoon break today. "I've got a bottle of aloe pomade you could try," Hortense said. "It works real good. It's made specially as a hair treatment."

Margaret was doubtful. She'd smoothed her hair that morning with a light dressing of rose-scented glycerin. Look what good that hadn't done. How could gunk called aloe help?

"After we finish these tables, if we ever finish these tables, we can run upstairs to the dormitory and put some on our hair," Hortense said.

"Nothing else has worked, so I'm willing to give it a try," Margaret said. "If we ever finish here."

They and the other waitresses still had to roll silverware, fold and stack extra tablecloths, and count out party favors, each for their respective assigned tables. Everyone had to be pre-prepared to redress tables that evening, as soon as the early dinner repast was cleared away. Then they all had to be on duty in the ballroom during the dance, and then had to rush back and serve midnight breakfast.

No one else in the room was finished, either, and it was already after two o'clock.

"What I would give to put up my feet for a spell, even for a few minutes," Margaret said. "If I can find a speck of shade out there that might be a touch cooler than in here, I will find ten minutes somehow, for a break before dinner. After we finish setting up the ballroom and after we finish setting up in here." She sighed and glanced out the nearest window to check the weather.

A slow horror began to dawn in her as she spied a fast-moving blur of black and white. *Oh, no, this will never do.* Not now, not today. Margaret stood glued in place, and stared.

"What in the world is that?!" exclaimed Hortense, following Margaret's gaze and looking outside.

Coming toward the main entrance, head up and footsteps strong, was Cousin Bridget. Her black veil and white underveil flew out and around her crown band and white wimple. They flapped in surrender to the breeze and the swirl of her black religious habit, which moved in concert with her rapid stride.

Cousin Bridget—Sister Mary Bridget—appeared to be a woman on a mission. Margaret suspected that mission stemmed from the housekeeper's refusal to release Margaret from work to attend Mass on the upcoming Epiphany Sunday. Nothing else would bring Bridget storming to the hotel like this without advance notice to Margaret.

If only she hadn't told Bridget about the final refusal of time off.

"Uh, that's my cousin," Margaret said.

"Oh!" Hortense said, and gave Margaret a perplexed, sidelong glance.

"Mercy, what will we see next in this place?" shrieked Arabelle, who stopped at the window when she scurried through the dining room with a pile of clean table linen.

If matters just couldn't get any worse, there was Francesco, driving up the wide, u-shaped entrance with a barouche full of new vacationers. By the looks of it, he was set for a collision with Bridget.

Margaret watched Francesco do a double take. He pulled on the reins and slowed the horses so Bridget could cross his path. For it was clear Sister Bridget had no intention of stopping.

A squeak of a cry escaped Margaret. She barreled past the astonished Hortense and the gaping Arabelle. She bolted out of the dining room and toward the parlor entrance, despite being prohibited this time of day. Servants weren't to be seen out of place. But she needed to ward off any potential confrontation between Bridget and management, and convince

Bridget to turn around and go home. Margaret could handle her own employment issues.

"Bridget, wait!" Margaret ran down the wide front steps of the porch and intercepted Bridget before she reached the building. Bridget halted, pulled Margaret into hug, and then released her.

"Margaret, I will not, cannot, leave my cousin to face this indignity without at least an attempt at intercession," Bridget said. "I've prayed over this and determined the best course of action."

"Uh, you mean about going to Mass, right?" Margaret asked, wishing for a sudden rain shower or a hard breeze that stirred up sandy dust, anything to divert attention away from this scene.

Francesco inched the barouche past the two of them. Margaret knew her face was a flame of color. It flushed in even the slightest of exertions and flooded when she was distressed. She forced herself to lift her gaze enough to acknowledge a hello to Francesco.

To her astonishment, his face shone with happy recognition.

"Good day to you, Sister!" he said, and took off his work hat and bowed his head briefly to Bridget. "It's a good day whenever one of the Lord's workers is a guest here. Allow me to be at your service for transportation. It's not every day I can be of use to a holy woman such as yourself."

"Walking keeps me fit, thank you," Bridget said. "And I'm not a visitor. I'm here to clear up this misunderstanding between Margaret and the management."

As if everyone knew about the problem, Margaret thought. They didn't. She'd kept it to herself. Why share trouble?

Vacationers gaped at Bridget. Margaret noticed some glance at her too. One murmured about the decline of society and problems with the help.

Francesco chuckled and mouthed the words "good luck" to her as he inched the barouche past.

"Do you see that servant's hair?" was the last thing Margaret heard as the barouche rattled toward the porch steps in front of the main entrance doors, just beyond Margaret and Bridget.

As passengers debarked, servants carried out pitchers of water and lemonade and placed them on tables between wicker chairs on the porch. Other workers set up a croquet court on the side lawn. They all craned to watch the unfolding scene while they hurried back and forth, as did disembarking guests.

"I feel responsible," Bridget said when Margaret tried to dissuade her from interfering. "I lined up this job for you and even encouraged you to move to Florida in the face of your mother's reluctance. Now you are barred from attending Mass. That is unthinkable. No, Margaret, I must speak to the manager—respectfully and with humility—but I must. As I noted, I've prayed about this."

She put her hand on Margaret's shoulder. "Never be ashamed of who you are, sweet Margaret."

Hearing those words voiced in the hotel's setting made them ring even truer. "I know, but it's hard, Bridget," Margaret said. She lowered her voice. "Most times people are nice in a work-like way, but I don't fit in, me with my brogue and my different religion and my clumsy hands and messy hair. Seems like it'll take me forever to learn the ins and outs of the job as good as any of them."

"And not a one of them is any better nor worse than you," Bridget said. She fixed a keen gaze on her cousin. "Now let's go find your supervisor and have a nice chat."

- - -

More than an hour later, Margaret and Bridget sat in the now-empty dining room, which was fully set for dinner except for the table Margaret had cleared for the two of them. No sense mussing anything. It'd be easier to re-set than re-clean.

Margaret watched the sun's afternoon rays shine through the window and illuminate tiny dust motes.

"How long does it take to attend to the management of one croquet party and an outdoor lemonade service?" asked Bridget. "I've said fifteen decades of the rosary."

"I'm sure Mrs. P is in no hurry to meet with us," Margaret said, and slouched into her chair as much as her corset would allow.

As the door creaked open, she straightened and Bridget turned her head. Something that appeared to be a walking mass of palm-tree branches topped by large palm fans moved into the room. Hands, then arms became visible as the fan-like sprays of greenery started to lower down. Finally, a full Francesco became visible.

He took off his cap and set it on the back of a chair rail. "Hello!" he called when he saw them. He deposited the rest of the greenery in a pile and strolled over.

"I volunteered to bring in these palm fans and set them up for tonight," he said, and looked at Bridget. "Now I see why: the Lord's hand at work, reminding me of my lapses. You said you're not a visitor. You live nearby? Is there a church nearby? I haven't attended Mass in I don't know when."

He glanced up, down, around the room. "Never expected to find Mass offered around here, but never asked, either. Just assumed there wasn't a Catholic church here."

Francesco sat down and, within minutes, learned that Persimmon Hollow Catholic Church was a mission parish, that a small church building had recently been erected in town, and that the local Catholic community's heart was centered at Taylor Grove, the acreage that housed the orphanage where Bridget and Margaret lived.

"The Taylors were early settlers and are leading citizens in town," Bridget said. "Their grove land adjoins the hotel's property. They actually built the orphanage."

Meet the Taylors in Book 1: _At Home in Persimmon Hollow_, which can be read as a stand-alone book.

"You live at an orphanage?" Francesco asked Margaret. "I have a lot to learn about Persimmon Hollow. All I know well is the hotel and the road between here and the railroad depot. I should venture into town more often." His tone betrayed a lack of enthusiasm.

"Everyone knows St. Isidore Orphanage," Bridget said. "The Taylors are generous benefactors. I gather you haven't met them yet. They have a citrus business and also own the tourist store by the railroad station."

Margaret waited for Bridget to finish. "Yes, I live at the orphanage," she answered Francesco. "Actually, I live in the convent. I forgot to tell you that when you asked if you could call on me."

Her heart skipped a beat. She didn't care that she'd reminded him. Bridget needed to know anyway. Besides, Margaret wanted to be sure Francesco meant it when he'd asked to call on her.

Bridget looked from Francesco to Margaret and back again, with a growing interest in her gaze. "I'm the superior at the orphanage. My order's small convent is within it. Actually, it's a part of it. We're blessed that Margaret decided to join us."

Francesco's smile faded.

"I see," he said. He scrambled up from his seat and retreated to the pile of greenery. "I need to get the fronds up on the walls." He wiped his hands on his pants and then through his hair. He looked at Margaret with puzzlement, then at Bridget, then at Margaret again. Shock settled on his features. He bent over and started collecting sprays of fan palms.

Clarity struck Margaret. "Francesco, I'm not studying on being a nun," she called to him. She stood up and put her hands on her hips. A puff of air escaped her scrunched lips. "I'm a guest there, a boarder," she said.

"Oh, goodness, I wasn't very clear in my explanation," Bridget said. A laugh escaped her, echoed by Margaret's.

Francesco straightened and turned around. Margaret's amused glance met his confused one. Seconds later, he laughed and returned to the table. "You had me worried for a moment," he said to Margaret. "I was wondering why you hadn't told me." He glanced toward Bridget. "Does this mean I have to ask your permission to call on Margaret?"

"You don't have to ask me, but it's a nice gesture and I appreciate it," Bridget said. "You're welcome to visit at any time. And to attend Mass with us in town, and join us for daily prayers, and for readings in our small chapel on the Sundays when we are without a priest."

Bridget's enthusiasm grew. "The others at the grove will be delighted to meet you and welcome you to the parish," she continued. "Why, we can make introductions this Sunday, before Mass. Afterwards, we'll gather for fellowship. As a mission parish, we aren't able to have Mass here as often as we'd like.

We're especially grateful Father will be here to celebrate Epiphany. Oh, this is wonderful. The Lord is good."

Francesco and Margaret exchanged uneasy glances united in mutual apprehension. Margaret knew where she and Francesco would be this Sunday: it wouldn't be in a pew at Persimmon Hollow Catholic Church or at an after-Mass picnic on the grounds of Taylor Grove.

"Can I help you put up the fans?" Margaret asked Francesco. "We're still waiting to meet with Mrs. P, and I have a feeling we'll be waiting a while longer."

"Sure, the more hands the better," he said. "If you could help hold the branches against the wall while I tack down the tops of the fans, that would be great."

"I'll pitch in too," Bridget said. She dug her timepiece out of her pocket. "We've been waiting well over an hour, but I'm prepared to outwait the housekeeper."

Francesco assessed the existing palm decorations that were starting to droop. "These need to come off first," he said. The three of them got to work. An hour later, finished, Francesco gathered up the dried sprays of palm fans, and put his hat back on. Mrs. P still hadn't arrived.

"What time is it?" Margaret asked.

"Just past four o'clock," Francesco said.

Bridget clucked, and a flicker of hope flamed in Margaret. Perhaps the housekeeper wouldn't show up at all. Dinner guests would start arriving in less than an hour. She had just enough time to run up to Hortense's quarters and attempt to tamp down her hair.

"It was nice to meet you," Francesco said to Bridget, and moved toward the door.

He stopped. "Margaret, I hope to visit tomorrow night," he said. "I figure the guests will be tired out from tonight and tomorrow's activities by then."

Margaret and Bridget waved farewells. "Bridget, I really should be going too," Margaret said. "It's almost time to serve dinner and I'm under orders to neaten my hair first."

They had avoided the dreaded meeting. Margaret was ready to add a skip of joy to her step.

"Oh, dear," Bridget said. "Well, you run along, and I'll wait."

She had no sooner spoken than Mrs. P strode into the room. The dust motes swirled in the air around her.

"How may I assist you?" she asked Bridget, without greeting her. She nodded at Margaret but didn't sit down at the table. Margaret watched the housekeeper look at the now-wrinkled tablecloth.

"I'll put out a fresh one before dinner guests arrive," Margaret said.

"You'd best hurry," Mrs. P said, and looked hard at Margaret's hair.

The scent of roasting turkey drifted through the room and reminded Margaret how hungry she was. There was no time left to eat, and long hours loomed ahead.

She made vain attempts to tame her hair while Mrs. P worked wrinkles out of the tablecloth. Bridget recited the same pleas Margaret had used in earlier requests for time off for Mass.

"We are more than willing to render to Caesar what is his," Bridget plunged on. "However, in matters of the soul..."

"Please, enough," Mrs. P said. "I regret we cannot accommodate your request. This is peak season and the hotel is booked full. I expect staff to understand the requirements of their jobs and adhere to them."

"Yes, of course, but..." Bridget was tenacious. "The previous manager promised me accommodations would be made for religious requirements for Margaret when she came to work here."

"The previous manager wasn't authorized to say any such thing," Mrs. P said. "In any event, that person no longer works here. As I told Margaret, the hotel management has graciously agreed to allow a preacher to conduct a Bible reading between mealtimes. That will have to suffice. I'm not aware of any guests of your religious persuasion here at the hotel. I suggest Margaret follow the examples of her coworkers and attend to her job duties, which are not yet up to our standards."

Margaret wondered whether she could find another position somewhere in Persimmon Hollow, before she got fired. Maybe as a live-in maid for a private homeowner, although she vowed she'd never do that again. Maybe a nanny. A companion. Anything!

Mrs. P ended the conversation before Bridget regrouped. "Excuse me," the housekeeper said. "A boating party will be back momentarily and expecting full maid and valet service before dinner. Others will expect the same between dinner and tonight's dance and celebration. This room also needs to be fully appointed for dinner guests before they start to arrive. That means no uninvited guests. Good day."

She departed with a swirl of her skirt and heavy steps across the wood floor. Margaret wished, just wished, that Bridget had let well enough alone. She hoped this intrusion wouldn't make her job any more difficult than it already was.

She hadn't told Bridget exactly how slow she'd been to learn the routines. How she still had trouble remembering to do things like serve hot dishes from the left and remove empty plates from the right. Or was it the other way around?

"Bridget, it's time for me to get this table and my workstation in perfect order."

"I'll continue to pray about this," Bridget said. She took Margaret's hands in her own. "Don't look so forlorn. We'll figure something out."

Margaret watched her go. She was dejected about missing Mass, but also about her lack of personal freedom and the mess she was making of her job.

She ripped the now-mussed tablecloth off and bundled it into a ball on the chair, went to her workstation and pulled out a clean one. She snapped it open in the air over the table, let it float down, and adjusted its placement with short, hard tugs and pulls.

It wasn't just the rigidity of the rules that bothered her. It was the way some people got to laze away the day at boating parties and croquet while she couldn't even grab an hour to worship the Lord in the companionship of her faith community.

She plopped down stoneware and cutlery with more force than necessary, and clanged the water pitchers as she set them out on tables. She didn't hear footsteps and gave a short jump when she turned and saw Hortense.

"Ah, Margaret, I came down before to bring you some of the aloe pomade but stopped when I heard you and your cousin talking with Mrs. P. I couldn't help but overhear."

Margaret felt her face flush and wondered if the day could possibly bring any more unwelcome surprises.

"Yes, I'm Catholic," Margaret said, and lined up the forks, knives, and spoons in perfect placement, although they were already neat. "Yes, I attend the Holy Mass and believe Jesus is in the Eucharist and I have a devotion to the Blessed Virgin Mary. I even talk to the saints sometimes. What do you have to say about it?"

"Nothing," Hortense said, and put up a hand. "I just wanted to say I'd be happy to cover for you Sunday morning. It's only for, what, an hour or so? These people almost never come down for early breakfast on a Sunday. Half our tables are always empty at that time. If by some surprise it gets busy, I'll get some of the others to help."

Margaret stared at Hortense's open, honest face, and felt her own stiff defenses relax. "Hortense! Thank you." She took a deep breath. "But I don't know. Mrs. P insists that guests like to see their usual servers."

"Pssfft," said Hortense. "They don't care and don't know one of us from the other. We're interchangeable to them."

- - -

Hours later, in crisp hat and apron, shined shoes, and tamed hair, Margaret stepped into the hotel's ballroom ready for duty as a beverage server for patrons who would sit at tables circling the dance floor.

She hadn't expected the vista before her. The wood-paneled room was transformed into a Florida orange grove, alive with real trees in massive urns. They lined the walls. Leafy citrus branches, some even bearing fruit, had been affixed to walls in artful representations of espaliers.

Gaslight in wall sconces cast just enough glow to make the room appear draped in moonlight. Even a large, round fabric moon, which hung in perfect balance from the rafters, had some kind of glow behind it that made it appear real.

"Wow is what I said, too, when we were finally done," said Francesco as he came through the doorway. He dragged in a laden, two-wheel cart and steered it toward a corner.

"You did all this?" Margaret asked. She helped push the cart, taking care not to muss her clean apron or dirty her hands.

"I and some others," Francesco said. "It's funny what a farrier-driver is asked to do sometimes. At the snap of fingers, I had to make an iron clasp to hold a light behind that moon up there."

It was the closest Margaret had heard Francesco come to a complaint. Unlike her, he was dusty and mussed. His blacksmith apron bore signs of the recent work. When he glanced at her, she saw, to her surprise, shadows under his eyes.

"It's all beautiful," she said. "I hope you can get some rest now."

He laughed. "Maybe a few snatched minutes. Some guests want to greet the New Year with a full-course meal on the shores of Lake Winnemissett. Even this hotel couldn't do that plus stage this ball. So, I have to take them with breakfast to the lake right after we ring in the New Year."

"We're serving breakfast in the dining room right after midnight," Margaret said. "It's part of the ball's schedule. Why can't they eat here like everybody else?"

"Some important people are more important than others," Francesco said.

They stopped the cart in an empty corner. Francesco unloaded bales of hay and arranged them around the wheels and base, making the cart part of the tableau. He propped full citrus baskets atop and around other bales that remained inside the bed of the cart.

"No wonder this cart was so heavy," Margaret said.

"Even I noticed the weight," Francesco said. "Nobody else could spare even a half hour to help. It's the first time I understood why others have been griping about more guests without more staff to serve them."

Margaret hated to see Francesco bowed down by the same weariness that infected her and so many others. His cheer had bolstered her and helped fuel her.

"We'll get through this like we get through every obstacle in this big new land," she said. "I want you to get some rest right now. No excuses."

"Sure! At once. Hours of it," Francesco said, but she detected a hint of his usual self in his voice. "Seriously, I'll have time to catch a few winks, then get cleaned up and get the horses ready by midnight," he said.

His glance toward her contained some bemusement and a lot of appreciation. "Thank you."

"For what?"

"For caring."

"Oh, 'tis nothing." She stumbled over her words.

"It means more than you think," he said as he touched her arm.

Emotions flooded Margaret. Her reaction to his touch told her what her brain hadn't fully wanted to admit.

Francesco lowered his arm. She met his gaze and knew her own was filled with hope and happiness. "You look pretty tonight, Margaret."

Warning bells rang in her.

"I mean," he hurried his words, "you look pretty all the time. But especially tonight."

Something deep in her felt he was sincere. Those same compliments one man might use as seduction, he used as heartfelt words.

Nonetheless, she needed to lighten the mood. The gaslight ambience was getting to her. "You noticed because my hair is finally in order, and for once you're seeing me before service, not after it."

"Yeah, I guess, that's it," he said. "No, I mean, uh. Never mind. Looking at you reminds me I'm not fit for a guest or supervisor to see."

Margaret let her hand rest gently on his arm for long seconds. "Francesco, you really did make me feel pretty when you said that."

He lifted her hand and gave it a quick kiss. The spark had returned to his eye. "Until later, then," he said.

"Bye," she waved as he left, and started to hum as she tidied errant tablecloth folds and neatened cutlery.

- - -

"Ten ... nine ... eight ..." Margaret got caught up in the excitement of the countdown. "...seven ... six ... five ..."

She moved near the door, to stay out of guests' way. But the night's magic had sprinkled its dust over her, and she called out the numbers with everyone else. "... four ... three ..." The door opened behind her, and Francesco slipped in, cleaned, scrubbed, and humor restored. He grabbed her hand and she gripped it tightly in return.

"... two... ONE!" Shouts of "Happy New Year!" rang out, noisemakers squeaked and banged, and people hugged in joy.

Francesco pulled Margaret to him and kissed her, right on the lips, in a quick, brief touch, then let her go. Their gazes locked. She saw a shy light of love in his, and wondered if it reflected her own, for she felt the same essence.

Quick as a dragonfly's dart, she pecked him back on the cheek, then blushed.

The smile on his lips matched the joy in his eyes. Margaret felt happier than at any time since she'd first arrived in this strange land of Florida. For the first time, the tumult that had sparked her flight released its grip, and happiness seeped in.

Chapter 5

January 1, 1892

As New Year's Day drew to a close, Margaret was actually home early for once. She settled into the bliss of relaxation. Even hotel guests had been tired from the late-night ball and early morning festivities. Dinner hours had been shortened, with a limited menu that allowed for faster service.

We should be so lucky every night, Margaret thought. She arranged crochet lace motifs on a fabric backing on a table in the orphanage's anteroom, which doubled as a sitting area and lobby for the chapel that opened onto it.

The orphanage had quickly become home to her, unlike the hotel and her job. She felt more comfortable here, amid the spare benches, tables, chairs, and pine wainscoting, than surrounded by plush and ornate hotel furniture. Each room provided her with a sense of belonging, from the plain dining room to the open kitchen and living quarters. Even more, everyone, not just Bridget, acted like family.

Margaret stepped back a few inches and envisioned the finished collar, then nudged the round motifs apart another quarter inch. She needed to make enough lace for cuffs too. They would add a special touch to her sister's First Communion dress in the spring, if she could get the adornments finished and mailed in time.

The clock on the mantel chimed nine times. Margaret stifled a yawn and swallowed a disappointment. She'd been home for an hour, but Francesco hadn't visited.

She wished he'd call, as he said he'd try to do this very night. Hadn't he kissed her at the stroke of midnight? She hadn't seen him since then, but the kiss had been real. It had felt right.

"Dear Mary, Mother of God, pray for me," she murmured. "Help me to grow wiser and recognize truth from falsehood, especially in the ways of love. I have found a man who is true and good, who I'm falling in love with, and who I think is starting to love me. Please, let this be true."

She sat down and angled the chair so she could peer out the window into the moonlit surroundings. She settled into the rhythm of making single and double crochet stitches in a lacework pattern, but every few minutes she looked up and searched for movement that might be Francesco coming down the road.

After a short while, her crochet hook stilled. She pinned her hopes on the shadowed landscape, and then she decided she was being silly, sitting by the window to watch for a maybe visitor.

Margaret called it a night and unpinned her hair to release the tightness in her temples. She shook her head so her curly tendrils fell over her shoulders and halfway down her back.

A squeak of a hinge signaled the opening of the chapel doors onto the anteroom. The room's stillness gave way to a jumble of muted talk and the patter of feet as the older orphans, Bridget and the orphanage's other sisters filed out from special evening prayers for peace in the new year. Bridget walked over to admire Margaret's lacework.

Everyone turned at a knock on the door. Margaret rose in haste to reach the door before one of the orphans did, but she was too late. It had to be Francesco out there. Who else would call at this hour?

Margaret sat back down, smoothed her skirt, and remembered her loosened hair. It was like being half-dressed. She wrapped her tresses around her hands into a loose bun and grabbed enough pins to produce a semblance of order. Then she tried to corral her shortened breaths.

"Who are you?" asked the not-quite-teen boy who fancied himself the house doorkeeper.

"Francesco Bartolomeo, at your service," Francesco answered in an equally serious tone. "I've come to pay my respects to Miss Murphy."

The boy let him in. "Margaret, it's for you!" he hollered as though she weren't a few feet away.

"What kind of name is Francesco?" the boy asked.

"Frank, you would say in English," he replied.

"Margaret, his name is Frank!" the boy shouted. His counterparts snickered. The sisters shushed them. The girls watched, wide-eyed and whispering, as Margaret stood and beckoned Francesco over to the table. He sat down and leaned back to stretch his shoulders.

"Apologies for the hour," he said. Margaret was surprised to see he was almost as physically out of breath as she felt.

"Four guests decided they wanted to hunt alligators and that it had to be tonight, as soon as it got dark," Francesco continued. "I drove them to the riverbank, but they got spooked. The woods around the river are thick and noisy with critters. The water was dark and unwelcoming."

The orphans and sisters moved closer to hear the rest of his story. It may as well have been a social hour than a courtship call, Margaret thought.

"Soon as they saw red eyes staring at them from the water, they jumped back into the wagon and told me they changed their minds," Francesco said. "Even I was a bit put off by how many gators swam close to investigate the shore doings. Eyes as far as you can see. I had to keep myself from guffawing, though. I guess nobody told the brave hunters what gator eyes look like at night."

"Wow, wish I'd been there," one of the boys proclaimed.

"Eeewwww, not me," replied a girl.

"You could have been hurt," Margaret protested to Francesco.

"Nah." He shrugged. "I know how to handle myself in the outdoors. Besides, I only drove to the river, and that was because the guests insisted. I had no intention of going out in the rowboats with them."

"I'm glad," she murmured, and felt the heat rise again in her cheeks.

"I'm glad you're glad," he said in a lowered tone, and their gazes met.

Margaret was certain sparks from the embers in the fireplace snapped between her and Francesco. Something heightened every movement and sound. The people, the chatter, everything else in the room receded.

"Bedtime, everyone," Bridget announced to the orphans. She clapped her hands and moved to form a line. The magical moment crashed. The orphans moved into order and followed the sisters into the hall, with Bridget guiding stragglers who craned their necks and wanted to stay.

The youngsters didn't go quietly.

"Is that her boyfriend!? Sister, is that Miss Margaret's boyfriend?"

"Is she gonna marry him?" asked another.

"He's taller than her. Did you see? He'll have to bend down to kiss her." The girls giggled at their speculations.

Flustered, Margaret picked up her slender crochet hook and yarn. She started to add a smaller-sized round to the point area of the collar.

"What's that you're doing?" Francesco inched his chair closer and leaned in. "*Bellissimo!*" he exclaimed. "Margaret, what is this?!"

"Irish crochet lace. Kenmare Lace is its proper name. I learned when I was a child. This is a collar for a dress. The smaller pieces will be sleeve cuffs."

"Do you make any to sell?" Francesco asked. "This is fine workmanship. Why are you waiting on tables at the hotel when you can do this?"

She gave him a crooked half-smile. "Because I can't make this fast enough or charge enough to support myself and pay back the—I mean, send money to help my family. I make things mainly for relatives and myself. These pieces are for one of my younger sisters. My cousin asked me to teach crochet to the girls here to add to their skills, so I do that too."

"Hmm." Francesco leaned back in his chair. The two front legs tipped up a few inches. He crossed his arms across his chest. "Let me think on this. Maybe you can develop this into a business."

"Don't waste your time," Margaret said, in a tone sharper than intended.

"Why not?" Francesco plopped the chair back down with a thud.

"Because I tried that already, and I was robbed." She gulped, picked up her work and bent her head to it. *Come clean about this, Margaret. It's a new year. Francesco isn't at fault here.*

"I was robbed by a man in New York, who pretended to be my beau." Margaret directed her attention to her work. Each word almost hurt as she spoke. "He had big plans for a crochet business for me. He was a good talker. I got caught up in the idea, and got my whole family worked up. I was so excited. He needed money to get us started and pushed me to act fast, said we had to do everything right away. I borrowed and begged every last available penny that every family member could spare."

She lowered her head, along with her voice. "In some cases, even money that couldn't be spared."

Her hands stilled on the lace. Francesco gently lifted them and cradled them in his. "What happened then?"

She almost choked, it was so hard to get the words out. "He disappeared, just vanished, with all the money."

She gripped Francesco's hands. The pain of the memory was still fresh.

"That's how I ended up here. Bridget found out what happened. Family news travels fast. This job came available and she knew I had to find a quick way to start paying back my debts. All I had done before was service and I wasn't able to find another position in that type of work."

She clamped her lips closed, not ready or willing to share the reason why.

The clock on the mantel ticked in the silence. Margaret withdrew her hands and collapsed back against the chair, as though deflated.

"Now you won't rest until every penny is returned," Francesco said.

Her gaze flew to his. "You understand?"

"I more than understand. I know others who have been, as the Americans say, fleeced. It happens to good people."

He rose and started to pace. "My blood rises at what you suffered at this man's hands. No, he's no man. He's a coward. A weasel. Cheaters of women are lower than low. Better that you found out before he claimed any more of you."

He sat back down and took her hands again. "I'm not a good talker about what's close in my heart, Margaret. But I have strong feelings for you in my heart. I am a protector. Not a man who will do harm. My word, once given, is good."

She stared hard at him. She wanted, so desperately, to believe and to trust him.

There wasn't anything glib or polished about Francesco. He didn't act one way with her and another way with others. She knew that. Had seen it. He was open and honest, a hard worker, a good man. And, oh, so attractive. A warm feeling came over her, a sense of calm and peace.

"I have feelings for you, too," she whispered to him. "I just need time, is all."

"Time is what we have," Francesco said. "Plenty of it. We'll support each other the whole time it takes for us to pay…. Wait, let me say this in proper English: To meet our financial obligations."

"When you put it like that, what else can I say?" She laughed.

"Now, show me how this works," he said, returning his attention to her lacework board, on which finished motifs were arranged. He leaned his elbows on the table.

"It's like this," she said, and pointed to each piece as she spoke. "Once I get the crocheted pieces arranged to my liking, I tack them together onto the fabric. Then I crochet looser weaves to connect these larger pieces, which are called flower motifs. Once it's all crocheted together, I snip away the tacking that holds the piece to the fabric."

She warmed to her explanation. "Look, a finished piece is like this." She opened the table's one drawer and pulled out a crochet lace mantilla veil that was made available to guests who lacked proper head attire for Mass.

She went to drape the veil on Francesco's hands but he pulled back.

"No, my hands are too rough."

"Nonsense, this is sturdy needlework. Just be careful how you handle it."

"Set it on the table and I'll touch it."

She laid it out and he gingerly fingered the edge. Margaret was struck by the contrast between the lace's fragile appearance and the thick strength of Francesco's hands. He was gentle as he lifted the veil and let it cover his other hand. She thought what it would be like for him to caress her so softly.

He set the veil off to one side, took her hands in his again, and leaned in. She moved in toward him. The only sound in the room was the gentle flicker of an occasional sprig of wood in the low fire. The only light was the dim circle cast by the kerosene lantern she had positioned near her work.

"You are as beautiful as the needlework you create, Margaret," Francesco said. "More so." With his thumb, he traced her jawline and tilted her head closer toward his.

Her breath caught and her heart beat so fast she feared it was as loud as the clock's chimes. He was going too fast.

She pulled herself back and turned up the lantern wick.

He stood up and wiped a hand over his face. "I apologize. I thought, because of how at midnight we—"

"We kissed, yes, I know," she said, in a voice that sounded fluttery. She had wanted this second kiss, waited for it since last night, and now she was uncertain, hesitant. But she did want his kiss. Panic from the past shoved at her.

"I don't usually act so *stupido*," Francesco said. "You told me what you suffered with that coward-thief, and then I act like a horse's behind."

"I liked our kiss last night," she said. "I need a slower pace, is all."

He stopped and looked at her with an intense gaze. "Any man who treated one of my sisters like I just did you, I'd throw that man out of the house with orders never to show his face again. If you wish the same for me, I understand."

"I don't," she said and leaned in toward him. "Francesco, that kiss last night was magical. I liked it. I like you. But it scared me a little, because of what happened not so long ago."

"I'm not that fool from your past," Francesco said. "I respect your needs. We'll move at whatever pace you decide."

He didn't know, she thought, there had been a fool more cowardly than the one who stole her money. Now wasn't the time to bring it up, either. She couldn't. The memories were too much, coming at her all at once. She'd tell him. Soon.

"Please, sit with me while I work a little longer," she said, and pulled the chair he had used closer to her own. She needed to convey how his closeness meant something to her.

They sat quietly as she crocheted another motif from the strand of thread.

"Have you thought about selling your work at the tourist store the Taylors own?" Francesco asked.

"A little, but I haven't really met the Taylors yet, other than a quick introduction to Mrs. Taylor here one day," Margaret said. "I've heard so much about them. They were out of town when I first got here.

Now I'm at the hotel fourteen hours a day. All I do is sleep here, it seems."

He leaned forward, let his forearms rest on his thighs and gripped his hands together for a few seconds before loosening them and gesturing as he spoke.

"The tourist season will be over before we know it," he said. "Maybe you could make pieces during the slow time, the summer, and be ready to show them at the store next season."

"Maybe, but I still have to earn money to send home during the slow season and all summer. I'm hoping someone in town needs domestic help. What'll you do at the hotel during off-season? You're lucky they asked you to stay on."

"I know. When I got here, it was off-season. The hotel was closed except for a few maintenance men. One of them left without warning, and that's how I got asked to stay. The work is mainly upkeep on the hotel. It leaves me enough time to do ironwork and study my English. I had to learn blacksmithing right off because the regular guy burned his hand and couldn't work. He stood there and told me what to do and I did it. I have a lot to learn."

"That's how you became a farrier?"

He looked down at his hands. "I can't call myself a farrier yet," he said. "I'm an apprentice with a long way to go. It's a good skill to learn, and I intend to master it."

She liked his bold determination and his dedication. It reminded her she'd once had the same, and could reclaim both.

She tilted her head to one side and narrowed her eyes. "Maybe you could practice by making simple items to sell at that store you mentioned. Things like andirons and candleholders."

He caught her gaze with his own in shared conviction.

"I like the way you think, Margaret. That's a fine idea."

"I could make collars, cuffs, even antimacassars." She warmed to the idea.

"Anti-whats?"

"Antimacassars. They're small, crocheted covers that you put on arms and backs of sofas and fancy chairs. They're decorative but also keep dirt off the expensive furniture. Their design doesn't have to be as fancy as on a collar or cuffs, so they'd be faster to make. Maybe the hotel would even want to buy them!"

"You and I, we make a good team," he said.

"That we do," she said. "Think what it'd be like to see our handiwork on display and for sale and bringing good income. I know what else! You could make horseshoes to sell at the livery stable, and parts for wagons and whatever else they might need."

He grimaced. "Maybe. I don't do so good in town yet."

He rubbed his hands on his thighs. "That time at the livery stable I told you about? When I was called a wop? As I was leaving, a man out front said that if I was smart, I'd keep my distance. I didn't answer, just started to ride away but kept my head high. Heard him say to his friend that 'Eye-talians need to learn to stay in their place. Or we'll put them there.' They both laughed. Not a friendly laugh, either."

A flicker of pain crossed his face, and was gone.

"A few people don't make a community," Margaret said. "I bet those men aren't even from here. It goes against everything Bridget says about Persimmon Hollow."

"They don't scare me," he said, a glint in his eyes. "Just the same, I want to find out more about town life before I head back. Get to know more people first. Find out who's who."

"Like the Taylors, and others in the church community," said Margaret.

"Yes," he said. "One step at a time. We'll reach our goals."

She toyed with her crochet hook. "Sometimes I feel like I can't afford to spin dreams. Not after what happened last time I did."

"Hard work isn't dreaming," Francesco said.

"Having an idea is far from making it real," Margaret said. "We'd need to start now, and earn money for supplies, to make things to sell. We can use all that spare time we don't have. If I find a free half hour a night, it's a lot. And it usually goes to some other chore like blacking my boots."

She lifted a foot to show her scuffed, ankle-high boots. "Even tonight, with extra time, I have chores. These need blacking or else I'll hear about it at the hotel. One of the laces is beginning to fray, and I best take a needle and thread to it before it worsens. I can't afford even the pennies for a new pair of laces."

She shrugged. "If I can't find time or money now, why will summer be any different? Rich people might have leisure then, but I won't. I'll need to work."

Francesco leaned back in his chair and watched her. "We'll find a way, Margaret. Have faith. In our plans. In us. In God."

She glanced at him. "I wake up each day with ideas and plans, but I lose energy by the time the last dinner table is cleared and I get home. Morning comes so early."

"File our ideas in your mind." He tapped his head with his fingers. "I will too. They'll wait there, for when the time is right. When we figure out all the details."

His steadfastness and tenacity bolstered her. She'd grown from her mistakes, she knew. She could recognize the difference between fraud and opportunity. "Yes, we will," she said. She'd failed once. She wouldn't fail again. If Francesco could face down bigots, she could muscle up perseverance.

The clock chimed ten times. Francesco rose, and Margaret walked with him to the door. He stopped and faced her.

"Sweet dreams, my Margaret." He touched his fingers to his lips and then to hers for the briefest of seconds. Their gazes locked, and Margaret knew she was standing on the edge of being completely in love.

Chapter 6

It didn't take long before members of the hotel staff knew Margaret and Francesco were sweet on each other.

"We've decided you make a good match," said Hortense. She and Margaret sipped tea from earthenware mugs in the servants' break room between breakfast and lunch.

"Well, almost all of us," Hortense added in a lower tone as Arabelle entered the room. She gave Hortense and Margaret a chilly nod and took a seat at another table. She became interested in the condition of her nails.

"Watch your back," Hortense whispered. "She fancies herself a beauty and I heard her say she wouldn't mind a winter flirtation with 'the foreigner' as she calls Francesco. She ain't happy to see him and you mooning at each other like little puppy dogs."

Margaret almost spit her tea back into her cup. Instead, she swallowed and coughed. "Is that how we look to others?"

Hortense giggled. "No, not really, but it's easy to see you favor each other." She sighed. "I do love a romance."

Margaret wasn't sure what was worse, being the object of speculation or being ignored as she'd felt at first. Right now, she'd prefer to fade right into the background, at least until after Epiphany. The fewer people who knew when she was and wasn't at work, the better.

Arabelle scraped her chair to make room at her table for a male colleague who beelined straight for her upon entering the room. Margaret soon heard tinkling laughter from Arabelle and chuckles from the fellow.

"She's pretty enough and turns the heads of guys," Margaret said. "Why waste her time on me and Francesco?"

"Partly because she hates for anybody to have something she doesn't," Hortense said. "Plus, she thinks it's okay to toy with Francesco because she knows she'll only be here a few months. I overheard her say as much. Not to me. She thinks she's better than the lot of us because she's from a fine family in Connecticut. Fell on hard times, they did, and now she has to work. My family, we've been scraping a living from rocky land for generations. No highfalutin' ways allowed."

Margaret only half-heard the stream of Hortense's gossip. She was trying to tamp down an unwelcome sting of jealousy. "Just let her toy with Francesco's affections," she muttered. "She'll have to be dealing with me then."

Hortense laughed aloud, which caused Arabelle and the man to turn toward Margaret's table. A short while later, the man left. Arabelle also rose. She gave Margaret an annoyed glance as she sashayed between the room's furnishings and chairs with a snap of her dress. She stopped at the table on her way to the door.

"Learn the difference between grits and hot wheat cereal yet?" she asked Margaret. She arched her eyebrows and smirked, and swished out of the room.

"Whatever did she say that for?" asked Hortense.

"I can't imagine," murmured Margaret, but her chest suddenly hurt. A patron she'd been serving for almost a week asked for grits every morning. Margaret had never seen nor heard of a foodstuff named grits. Nor did she want to ask any of her colleagues. She didn't want to make herself look even more ignorant than she already felt about the job.

Each day, she had guessed what kind of porridge the gentleman really wanted, and scooped from the kettle that she'd assumed was grits. She suspected she'd been guessing wrong.

The next morning, Thursday, she stared at the kettles lined up before her in the kitchen. Her hands grew clammy. One porridge looked like oatmeal, another kettle held a cooked mixture of small, brown grains, and the third had what looked like the pablum given to babies up north. That one surely couldn't be the grits. It was obviously farina.

Margaret glanced around at other staff members buzzing at their work. She was slow enough to learn her job, as the housekeeper was wont to remind her. But she took a deep breath and swallowed her pride. It was only a question, after all. About porridge. She would ask.

Arabelle sauntered up and started to spoon cut fruit into serving dishes barely two feet away at the next counter. Margaret's question stuck in her throat.

"Hurry up, I've got a ferocious foursome, hungry as raccoons out there," said a harried staff member close behind her. Margaret scooped out a serving from the kettle with the dark grains, same as she'd done each day. She grabbed containers of cane and sorghum syrups, hoisted her tray, and hurried out to the dining room.

Sweat droplets formed on her forehead when she saw the housekeeper frown, glance her way, and then turn again toward Arabelle, who simpered something in the housekeeper's ear.

Margaret set the dishes on the table and turned to see the housekeeper only steps away.

"Is everything satisfactory?" Mrs. P sweetly asked the diners. Margaret held her breath.

"Best hot wheat cereal I've ever eaten," said the man who'd asked for grits. His companions conferred about the desirability of their victuals.

Heart hammering, Margaret tried to remain poised and calm as she waited for the rest of grits-man's statement to bring down calamity on her head. But he didn't utter a word of complaint. Nothing about not having ordered wheat cereal. Nothing about inept servants.

"Glad to hear it," Mrs. P said, and glided away with a look of reproof toward Arabelle, who slunk away in the other direction.

Grits-man chuckled and snapped his napkin onto his lap. Margaret rushed to inquire if he wished for anything else.

"Grits are a small-grained porridge that resembles the pablum served to invalids and babies," he whispered to Margaret. She flushed but her glance spoke a world of thanks to him. "You serve it with butter or syrup," he added. Then he spoke up. "All is well here, my dear. Thank you."

She curtsied and almost ran to the kitchen, her faith in the wider world a tiny bit restored.

- - -

Francesco guffawed and Bridget grinned when Margaret relayed the incident to them that night as they sat in the wicker chairs outside the orphanage. The hour ticked past ten, but the night air was like a cool sateen wrap. The scent of jasmine hung around them. Margaret even smelled early citrus blooms, a new scent to her and one that intoxicated with its sweetness.

"I'm going to make sure he has a double serving of grits tomorrow and every remaining day of his stay!" Margaret said.

"Be sure to alert whomever serves him during your absence at Mass on Sunday," Bridget said. "Such a kind man."

Bridget turned toward Francesco. "Will you be able to join us Sunday morning?"

Francesco, whose gaze had leveled on Margaret after Bridget's comment about Margaret's absence, gave Bridget his attention.

"I have to usher an early-morning hunting party to the quail grounds on Sunday. It's already on my work schedule."

"The Lord will understand," Bridget said. "I'm heartened that Margaret's housekeeper saw fit to release her for Mass after our little talk the other day. Especially now that we're relying on Margaret to play the melodeon at church."

Francesco sent a questioning look in Margaret's direction. She saw it even in the dim glow of lantern light spilling out from the orphanage front window.

"You know, it was a long day and I'm tired," Margaret said. She stood up and stretched. "I'm going to turn in. The weekend will be busy. The housekeeper said the hotel is fully reserved and dozens more guests arrive tomorrow."

"Perhaps we could take a short walk for a few minutes, to smell the beautiful flowers?" Francesco said. He gestured toward the closest jasmine bush, whose small, white, star-like blossoms glimmered in the moonlight.

"A delightful idea," Bridget said. "I'll wait here."

Margaret glowered at Francesco, but he stood and reached out his arm.

"This way?" he asked, ever so casually, and indicated the shrubbery. She grudgingly let him take her arm.

He released her when they were out of Bridget's hearing, although not out of sight.

"You could get fired! What are you doing?!"

"I got stuck, okay? Bridget thought I had the time off before Mrs. P said absolutely no. The church needs a melodeon player and I had already said yes. Hortense said she'd cover for me." Margaret's words tumbled out. "Most important, I want to attend Mass. They have no right to say I can't go. It's not fair." She put her hands on her hips. "I don't have to be answering to you anyway, Francesco."

"I know," he said.

"So why are you all huffy?" she asked.

"I'm not, as you say, huffy. I'm worried. You're lying. If Mrs. P finds out, you could be without a job. I know it's not fair that you can't go. But it's the way things are right now. Life's not always fair."

Margaret bit her lip. "I'm not lying," she said. She had let slide her cousin's mistaken assumption that the housekeeper had granted time off. "I'm just not saying everything."

"Tell your cousin the truth," Francesco urged. "You heard her say the Lord will understand."

"No."

"Why not? This makes no sense!"

"Partly because I want to attend Mass. Partly because I'm mad at the way some of them treat me at the hotel, as if I'm second-class—some dumb newcomer who can't grasp the complexities of an American job. On top of that, some of them have said hurtful things about my being Catholic, soon as they saw Bridget at the hotel, as if I can't figure out the job because I listen to the Pope. Like he's here telling me to drop dishes and mess up grits! I try to ignore the remarks, but it's hard."

Francesco ran his hand through his hair. "I understand, believe me. On all counts."

She relaxed her shoulders a bit and blew out a breath. "I didn't realize how important Mass is to me until I started having to miss it after moving here. The priest only gets here every couple of weeks."

"You say someone offered to cover for you?"

"Yes, Hortense offered. You've seen her. She and I share a workstation in the dining room."

He nodded his approval. "Nice of her."

"Yes, it is. Can't you get someone to cover for you?"

He shook his head. "There aren't enough of us in the stables right now. And I'm not sure I'd disobey a direct order from my boss even if one of the other fellows stepped in for me. Who knows what will happen to you if the housekeeper finds out about your scheme."

Margaret didn't like to acknowledge the risk. In her mind, the housekeeper was stubbornly rigid, and she, Margaret, had every right to do as she planned.

"I'm willing to take a chance. Hortense and I think it won't be any problem. I'll start work at five-thirty to serve the early risers, and then slip out at six-thirty to ride to town with my cousin. She's arranged for someone to bring me back right after Mass. I won't get to mingle and have coffee and biscuits with everyone but—"

She grabbed Francesco's hands as though willing strength to flow from them to her. "Everything will be fine. I'm certain. As long as nobody snitches on me."

"Why would anybody do that?" He squeezed her hands before she lowered them. Together they strolled back to the front of the orphanage, holding hands and walking side by side. Bridget smiled and looked away for a minute as Francesco kissed Margaret on the cheek in farewell.

Margaret reviewed the plan for Sunday in her mind as she prepared for bed. No one would find out. She was sure of it.

Chapter 7

Margaret stretched her little finger until it ached. Her fingertip just reached the smallest bass button on the melodeon. Why had she agreed to play this bulky box at Mass tomorrow?

She squeezed out a few wheezy notes. *This would never do.* Margaret took a breath, adjusted the instrument's shoulder strap, and straightened her posture. She took a furtive look around the orphanage's dining room and listened for footsteps. Good. No one was near, not in the middle of the afternoon. All were at tasks, prayer, or schoolwork.

Never had "Holy God We Praise Thy Name" sounded so pained. Margaret struck more wrong notes than right ones. Only when a shadow fell over her did she look up from her focus on finger placement.

Bridget stood there, hands on hips, and winced at the sounds wheezing from the instrument.

Margaret offered a half-smile that carried more than a hint of apology.

"My ambition to help with music at Mass exceeds my ability," she said.

Bridget didn't disagree. "God blesses each of us with different talents, Margaret. You have a lovely voice. Why don't you plan to sing instead? We'll make do with the instruments we all have—our vocal chords."

Margaret made haste to remove the melodeon strap and set the instrument aside. "Thank you! What a relief."

If only she felt relief about the other matter weighing on her conscience. She needed to come clean about the truth of her time off. She should tell Bridget she'd arranged the absence without approval.

Margaret considered the idea for less than a minute, then brushed the thought away. Wouldn't God rather she attend Mass instead of serve flapjacks to people who didn't frequent church?

She glanced at the clock on the wall. "My break is almost over," she said. "I better get back to the hotel. The housekeeper said be ready to serve a full house again tonight."

Bridget walked with Margaret out to the hallway. "What is your plan again for tomorrow? Early to work, then back here to ride to town with us? Will you still need immediate transportation back here after Mass?"

"Oh, yes, the sooner the better."

Bridget gave her a quizzical look. "Odd that the hotel won't spare you an extra half hour for fellowship."

Margaret gave her a tight smile and slipped out the door before Bridget could ask any more questions.

The day went downhill from there. Margaret's nerves frayed in accord with the quickened pace of work throughout dinner. The hotel wasn't just full, it was beyond capacity, in her opinion.

Margaret squeezed between chairs and rushed to accommodate the two extra tables pushed into her service area. "Yes, sir, the coffee is brewing," she said to the man who sat with a raised cup in his hand while she twisted the pepper grinder over salads at the adjacent table.

"One moment, ma'am. Yes, your main course will be out in a minute," she said over her shoulder to another table, where salad plates sat empty but for bits of wilted lettuce. Could she push herself any faster? Heading toward the kitchen, she almost collided with Arabelle, who scowled at her.

The kitchen was a swirl of people, movement, heat, smoke, and mingled scents of roasted poultry, sweet potato casserole, and other cooking aromas. She grabbed plated entrees and powered back to the dining room. Dropped those off, poured coffee, took the orders of the newly seated group. The tasks strung along a line in her mind and pushed all other thoughts away.

Three long hours later, the last diners gone, Margaret collapsed into a chair and surveyed the post-meal ruin across the table. She picked up an edge of the tablecloth, draped it over the mess, and pushed it toward the middle so that a corner of the table was clear. She leaned over, rested her head on her hands, and closed her eyes for a weary moment.

Lord, please let the breakfast crowd be small and quiet, much, much smaller and quieter, she pleaded. Please let no one notice my absence tomorrow morning.

She straightened and faced the task at hand. Nobody else was going to clean her section. As she started to rise, the tablecloth caught between her knee and the table leg, and caused the pile atop the table to slide. Before she could stop it, a dessert plate plunked on the floor. A fork clattered down right after, as if to confirm that yes, once again, Margaret Murphy had messed up on the job.

Margaret picked up the plate, now chipped. She retrieved the fork and looked around to see if her latest transgression had been noticed. Unfortunately, yes. A few colleagues, while laboring at their own cleanup tasks, glanced her way. Everyone looked as exhausted as she felt. She plodded through the remainder of her chores, too tired to worry about ramifications.

The moon was high and it was near midnight when she finally crossed the railroad tracks and plodded toward the orphanage. At least she'd get a few hours of sleep. She wondered how much would be removed from her pay envelope for the broken dish.

Margaret no longer cared that she had bent rules to get time off for Mass. Not after how overworked and pushed she and the others had been tonight. She needed the respite.

She inhaled the jasmine scent as she walked past the bush laden with blossoms and wondered how Francesco was faring. She hadn't seen him, since they'd all been so frantically busy. But the thought of him made her smile and softened her fatigue.

- - -

Sunlight streamed through the oval stained-glass window that was one of the treasures of Persimmon Hollow Catholic Church. The tinted rays illuminated the small, wooden church's interior with jewel-like richness. The congregation's blended voices struck harmonious notes as the Mass processional began.

Margaret inhaled the incense and blessed herself twice in response to the priest's *Dominus vobiscum* greeting, so glad was she to be in attendance.

She lowered her head and spoke to God with fervor when Father said *Oremus*, an invitation to prayer, after the Gloria. Thank you Lord, she whispered in her heart, for helping me get here. Then she gulped. As if God had told her to sneak out of work and lie about it.

She'd been relieved to learn, from the few guests at her dawn table service, that some patrons had dined even earlier at an outdoor hunt breakfast, and that many others were en route to the hotel's lake pavilion. A special event was planned, which included lakeside breakfast, boating, tennis, and a picnic lunch.

Hortense had given Margaret a thumbs-up and a friendly nod when she slid away at six-thirty. The sky to the east was a blush of rose and peach, and mockingbirds trilled to greet the morning sun. As she hurried to the orphanage to catch a ride in their wagon, Margaret thought of a verse she often heard Bridget use when leading the children in morning prayer:

Cause me to hear thy mercy in the morning; for in thee have I hoped. Make the way known to me, wherein I should walk: for I have lifted up my soul to thee. (Psalm 142:8*)

Now at Mass, she felt she was exactly where she was supposed to be, at least for today. At the end of the Prayer of the Faithful, she added her own plea that God help her find and stay on the path meant for her. She prayed for special blessings for Francesco. He must have risen in the middle of the night to start transporting equipment, food, and people to the breakfast sites.

Then she knelt and bowed her head and heart for the Liturgy of the Eucharist.

When Margaret made her way back to her pew after receiving Communion, she noticed hotel guests in the first row. The group included the man to whom she'd served the wrong breakfast for days. What a nice surprise, to see them here, to know at least a handful of hotel patrons were Catholic.

Margaret soaked in the shared togetherness with them and with everyone at Mass, and in the blessing that came from feeling the presence of Christ in her heart. Back in her pew, she quietly lowered the kneeler, got to her knees, and prayed deeply.

- - -

Margaret returned to work with gratitude and lightness in her heart. She carried renewed determination to master the practical and social skills needed to handle her job. She looked around the hotel yard and toward the stable before she ran inside the main building, and felt a tug of disappointment. Francesco's regular wagon was nowhere in sight. Still out with the hunting party or lakeside excursion, she supposed.

She re-pinned her starched cap to her flyaway hair and hurried toward the dining room. Her senses were on sharp alert. Francesco, she wanted to see. Mrs. P, not so much.

Inside the dining room, scattered guests at tables here and there sipped tea and coffee, and nibbled on pastries and fruit cups. The scene in no way resembled the frantic activity of the night before. A few men read newspapers while they ate with leisure. Why, Hortense was even lining up clean water glasses on their shared workstation. No one ever had time to do that during meal service.

"Here, I'll finish," she said, and took over the glassware organization. "I can't thank you enough, Hortense. How did everything go?"

"It was so empty in here, like I've never seen it," Hortense said. "Had both of us been here, we might have been bored."

"I'm sure Mrs. P would have found something for us to do," Margaret joked. "Uh, has she been here?"

"Nope. Rumor says she went out to personally supervise the lakeside breakfast."

"Whew." Margaret felt guiltily happy at the ease with which she'd pulled off her absence. But her act of direct disobedience at work tugged at her conscience. Definitely something to clear with the Lord at confession, she knew.

"I'm glad everything worked out for you," Hortense said.

The hand of friendship was encouraging to Margaret. Maybe people were starting to see her as a person, instead of the foreign Irishwoman who lived with her own kind, couldn't do her job, and was only temporary help.

The morning's radiance remained with her through the main Sunday dinner, despite being busy. Mountains of game had been sent to the kitchen with the return of the hungry hunters and had been transformed into savory dishes. Margaret was exhausted but content when she finally slipped away in early evening. Supper had been light and ended early, with many guests tired and absent after the long day and heavy midday dining.

Margaret hoped Francesco had a break that evening too. Her heart quickened when she saw the wagon he usually drove parked inside the open barn door. She detoured into the stable area. It was clean and quiet, the animals were fed and brushed, and the wagons and barouche washed, wiped down, and polished.

But Francesco wasn't there. Odd. He was in and out of the stables so much that he often noticed her leave the main building. He'd head over to intercept her, if only for a quick hello.

Exiting the barn, she looked around the grounds. Some couples strolled the bamboo walk, a winding path that led to a bathhouse and cement pool. Other people relaxed in rocking chairs on the hotel's long front veranda. A few musicians—two violinists and a flautist—tuned up in the gazebo, around which chairs had been placed in a semi-circle. Lighted candles in staked holders cast a soft glow in the waning daylight.

The scene was tranquil and pretty. For once, Margaret felt honored to be a staff member at such a notable destination. She wanted to share the moment with Francesco. Where was he?

After a quick but fruitless search, she abandoned hope. Francesco must have gone straight to his quarters, and male quarters were off-limits to female staffers. How tired he must have been, she thought, and her own weariness tugged in sympathy.

Swallowing the minor setback to her joyful day, she started to circle the other side of the stable area and return to the orphanage. Outside, on the far side of the barn, was Francesco.

She stopped mid-step and set down her foot on the ground with quiet pressure. Francesco sat on the grass, knees up and arms resting on them, and with his head leaning back against the outer wall. He was sound asleep. Margaret could see the fatigue etched into the smudges of sandy grit on his tanned face. His hair was mussed, and his clothes wrinkled and showing the dirt of the day's labors. The cap he liked to wear was on the ground, upside down, as though it had fallen from loosened fingers.

Margaret avoided stepping on oak leaves, pine straw, twigs, or anything that would crinkle or snap and wake him. No one should have to work to the point of exhaustion, she thought.

She wanted to sink down and nestle in next to him. Instead, she tiptoed past, blew him a kiss, and said a prayer of healing for him. Then she said one of thanks for herself, that her day had gone exactly as planned. She was certain she'd escaped trouble.

Chapter 8

The bright sun beamed a sharp contrast to Margaret's dark mood the next day.

"Mrs. P did what?" Francesco pushed his hat farther back on his head and looked down at Margaret. He leaned one hand and arm on the rail of the wagon he was cleaning.

"She said she was dismissing me to give me time to think about my errors. That she doubted my ability to 'perform my job duties to the level of perfection required by the management.' That she wasn't sure she will call me back to work."

Margaret rolled the edges of her apron in an endless loop. The coins she'd been sending home were meager indeed, but they helped add scraps of meat and day-old bread to the table. They helped pay the rent, late though it usually was.

She knew if the family's rent fell behind even more, they'd be forced from their lodgings. Because of her. "Right now, I'm just trying to figure out what to do next."

The apron fabric was a twisted mess all along its ruffled edges.

Francesco frowned. He resumed wiping oil soap onto the wooden railings with precise movements. "I'll think on it, too. Don't worry. We'll come up with something. How did Mrs. P find out about you leaving for church? Did somebody snitch?"

"No. That's what I first thought too. I blamed Arabelle. I was certain she'd said something. But it wasn't her. The guests I saw at church made a comment to Mrs. P about how nice she was for allowing her staff to meet their religious obligations."

Francesco hooted. "I bet she had trouble answering that!"

"I would guess yes. But she was incensed that I disobeyed her direct order." Margaret swallowed. "And I was annoyed because I knew she was right about that. Then Mrs. P mentioned the latest dish I chipped. Apparently, she started asking about the dish and a couple of people finally admitted what they saw. Mrs. P said the two transgressions were the last straws. She ordered me out in front of everyone. It was humiliating."

Margaret could still feel the stares. Hortense had given her hand a quick squeeze as she passed. Arabelle smirked. Others had watched with expressions that anticipated new gossip to fill their day.

"I feel a little better now that I'm outside, with you," she said. "But I have to figure right away how to keep helping my family. They rely on me. Maybe I can ask Bridget for a loan. No, she hasn't anything to spare. Oh, I dread even telling her. She never does anything foolhardy."

Francesco paused his polishing. "Come on." He put down his rag. "This cleanup here can wait. I don't have anything on schedule until after lunch. Let me walk you back to the orphanage."

He took her hand in his. His concern, his love, his care were balms for Margaret's hurting heart. She looked up at him, her soul alive in her eyes.

He did a quick movement of surprise, took a step back, and then moved toward her. "Can I speak freely, really freely?"

"Of course! It's one of the things I admire about you," she said.

"If I could ask you to spend your life with me starting today, Margaret, I would." His gaze was direct and intense, and his words honest. "That day will come, I promise. I want to help you shoulder your burdens, now and forever. Will you consent to be my wife?"

Margaret's mind swirled and her heart swelled. He gently drew her to him, and she let her hands come to rest against the warm firmness of his chest. His arms went around her. She leaned in as he pulled her tight against him. His lips found hers and she sighed with a bliss that dulled some of the troubles that haunted her.

They broke apart after the sweet kiss.

Margaret gazed up at him. "I think, no, I know, I'm falling in love with you, Francesco. But I need more time. I'm not ready to say a forever yes."

His gaze dimmed but he accepted her words.

"We haven't known each other for very long, but I feel like you're both my beau and my best friend wrapped into one," Margaret said. "It makes me feel strong. It's not that I can't see us together in the future. Oh, I can! But there's a lot I must do first."

"You put things into words better than I do," he said. "Maybe we start planning our future now, even though it will take time to get there. It's good to face the world with the right person at your side. We'll stand together, you and I. And anybody facing Sister Bridget needs support. Let's go. I won't leave you."

"My dear cousin won't cover me in pity, that's for sure," Margaret said.

The kiss, his words about their future, his love, and his closeness all helped dull the aching knot in her stomach. Together, they would find the way forward.

- - -

At the orphanage, Margaret's earlier dismay gave way to petulance. Bridget was annoyingly nonjudgmental. At the same time, she prodded Margaret's conscience.

"She's good," Francesco whispered from behind Margaret.

Margaret scowled.

"I don't want to apologize to the housekeeper," she said to Bridget.

"Just a suggestion," Bridget said. "Above all, put yourself in the Lord's hands. Go to confession as soon as possible. I also recommend you say an Act of Contrition, immediately."

"You would," grumbled Margaret. Francesco let out a low whistle, followed by a "whoa." Bridget's eyes widened.

"Our family is known for squaring off in the face of one another's stubbornness," Bridget told Francesco, without taking her gaze off Margaret. "My dear younger cousin is well aware of what she must do. That's why she's frowning."

Margaret wrestled with her feelings, which roiled inside with the turbulence of the waves she remembered from crossing the ocean. She stood, arms crossed over her chest and lips pressed together. A hint of movement outside the nearby window caught her attention. She turned her head in that direction. Outside, a wren hovered over the bowl affixed to a statue of St. Francis. A bigger mockingbird swooped in, chased it away, and flew off. The wren returned. Again, it fluttered off after the mockingbird landed beside it. Moments later, it returned. Suddenly, the two birds pecked seed side by side.

Persevere, Margaret, persevere.

She returned her gaze to the concerned faces of Bridget and of Francesco, who had moved and now stood next to Bridget.

"I'll go talk to Mrs. P and tell her I did some thinking," Margaret said. She walked over to the table on the far side of the room and opened the small center drawer. She withdrew her needles, hooks, a half-crocheted sleeve cuff, and small ball of yarn.

"In the meantime, maybe we could plan to pay a call on the Taylors. Maybe they'll be interested in some crochet lacework for their tourist store." She glanced at Francesco. "And maybe they'll be interested in some trivets, andirons, hooks, or other ironwork that Francesco might be willing to supply."

"You know I'm going to marry that girl someday," he said to Bridget.

"I didn't formally say yes yet," protested Margaret. But her heart knew the answer, and she glowed within. "Okay, yes."

"After a suitable courtship," Bridget said. "You two hardly know each other." But she appeared pleased.

"A woman learns a lot about a man when she sees how he works day in and day out," Margaret said.

"Same goes for a man learning about a woman," Francesco said.

"But you're right, as usual," Margaret told Bridget. Peace began to flow in her again. Maybe St. Francis and the birds had something to do with it. Or St. Anthony. Could one pray for help in finding lost peace and optimism? Why not?

She was determined to overcome obstacles in her path. The hunger she'd seen in the eyes of her siblings was never far from her mind. Her responsibility for returning to them what she owed weighed heavy. She'd not leave them in need.

"We're not going anywhere quickly, Bridget," she said. "We both have much to do. I'll work until my fingers bleed to help the family, doing anything honest I can find. I'd like to hold my head up in the community here, again, as well."

"I have months left before I'm free of my obligation to my *padrone*," Francesco added. "Margaret knows all about that. Only after the contract ends will I be my own free man. I hope to start my own blacksmith business."

"Have you thought of starting it in Persimmon Hollow?" Bridget asked. "As far as I know, we have only an itinerant blacksmith. A settled business would be welcomed, I'm sure."

"Yes, but I have to weigh how the townspeople might react to me first."

He filled in Bridget on his experience at the livery stable.

She narrowed her eyes. "Very unusual for Persimmon Hollow. I'll ask around about who those men might have been. If I had to guess, I'd say they were just passing through."

"I'd start slow and build up the business, but yes, it is a dream I have," Francesco conceded.

"You have time to consider," Bridget said. "Margaret also needs several months to pay back her debts. That way you can start life together unencumbered."

Margaret and Francesco held hands and let the idea soak in.

"A local blacksmith shop, that's something else to talk to the Taylors about," Francesco said to her. "They might know the best location."

"Let's see how soon we can meet with them," Margaret added.

"After you talk to the hotel housekeeper, of course, and apologize, and with God's grace maybe get your job back," said Bridget in that calm voice that infuriated Margaret sometimes. "Lies and omissions never come to any good."

Margaret resisted the urge to roll her eyes. "I know, Bridget. I think I've learned my lesson."

Francesco squeezed her hand. "The future will be grand."

But first, Margaret knew she had to fix the present.

- - -

The next morning, Margaret was summoned back to the hotel before she had a chance to rehearse what to say to Mrs. P or inquire about a meeting with the Taylors. She dressed in her uniform, just in case, grabbed the first kerchief she could find, and wrapped a crocheted shawl around her to ward off the unusual hint of chill in the air. Florida could go from hot to cold overnight in winter, and then back again.

She was just outside the orphanage when she saw Francesco rattle down the sandy roadway in a mule-drawn work cart.

"I came to give you a ride over, soon as I heard they were looking for you," he said when he pulled up beside her. "This counts as work."

"Thanks! How did you hear?" Her breath came out in puffs in the cold air.

"The housekeeper told Hortense, who told me. I think it's a good sign, the way they're looking for you."

Margaret sunk into her thoughts until the hulking façade of the hotel loomed up before she was ready to see it. Nerves jumbled in her stomach. She untied the kerchief she'd put on to keep her hair in place.

"Did Hortense say what Mrs. P wanted?" she asked. Francesco hopped down and came around to her side of the cart.

"No, just for you to be here as soon as possible."

Questions flew away as he put his hands on her waist to help ease her off the bench seat onto the ground. She liked the way he was so gentlemanly. And the way his hands felt on her. Her heart, already aflutter with anxiety, beat rapidly anew.

"Thank you," she said as she smoothed her uniform. "For the ride and for everything."

"Be brave, Margaret." He climbed back in and started to inch the cart away from the front entrance.

"I'll be over there in a little while." He pointed toward a shady spot near the servant work area. "I've got to transport a lunch party later, and the food and tents and other supplies will come out over there."

Margaret said a Hail Mary, and then another one, and marched up the front steps as though entitled to do so.

Inside, as soon as she stepped through the doorway, she saw Hortense rush down the stairs with a broom and dustpan. What was she doing with maid tools? Margaret didn't have time to ask, and Hortense didn't stop. She signaled Margaret to follow.

"Special staff meeting, starting right now, and Mrs. P told me she wanted you to be there, too," she said over her shoulder, her pace quick. "As if I have time for this. I hope it's a short meeting."

Margaret followed her down the hall and into the dining room. She wasn't sure she was even on staff anymore.

The meeting was just starting as they entered. Mrs. P nodded as they took the first open seats available.

"As I was saying, I realize how busy you all are, so I'll be brief," the housekeeper said. "I wish to announce staffing changes, effective immediately."

Margaret gulped. She was about to be fired for good, in front of the entire workforce.

The housekeeper read a short list of names and duties and changes in responsibilities. "Also, Arabelle will no longer serve as a substitute wait staff where needed. She will permanently take over the southeast service corner of the dining room and will share a waitstation with Hortense."

What a way to be fired. If only her cheeks wouldn't flame so much, Margaret thought, no one would notice her distress. Her fingers curled into fists underneath the cover of her apron.

"Margaret, who formerly served in that capacity, will now join the outdoor serving staff. She will accompany parties who wish to picnic for breakfast or lunch. That is all. You may return to your posts."

Margaret stood up and then sat back down, stunned. Others flowed around her in all directions as they rushed back to their duties. Arabelle simpered and smiled at Mrs. P and Hortense looked glum. Margaret could hardly believe she wasn't fired. Her family wouldn't be out on the streets. She could continue sending money home. She said a quick prayer of thanks.

The housekeeper beckoned Margaret.

"Margaret, consider this your last chance," she said, as she led the way back toward the kitchen. "I don't grant it lightly. But we need all hands this season. There are fewer things to break on picnics, and dining protocols are slightly loosened."

She delivered Margaret to the cook. "You'll take your direct orders and schedule from her." The housekeeper looked meaningfully at the cook. "You will report any problems to me." The cook replied with a serious yes, and the housekeeper departed.

"She doesn't know it," the cook said to Margaret, with a nod toward the retreating supervisor, "but you just joined the best team at the hotel."

Chapter 9

Several weeks later, Margaret stood in a picnic setting that was new to her, and magnificent: an open, grassy expanse dotted with massive live oak trees. Spanish moss dripped almost to the ground from some of the limbs. The lake beyond was a jewel-like blue, reflecting the bright sky dotted with puffy clouds.

Still, Margaret couldn't believe the heat and humidity. It was late February, and hard to believe that up north her relatives shivered under gray skies and snowy winds.

This steam bath is good for the skin, if nothing else, she told herself about the sheen on her face. A tiny drop of sweat beaded off her nose. She frowned at Francesco as she patted her cheeks and forehead with a towel. "The cook said this was the best team, but she didn't say it was the hottest team."

He cast her a glance of understanding as he offloaded a hamper of food and boxes of supplies from the wagon.

"I'll unpack them in a minute," Margaret said. She fanned herself in the shade of the long, thick arms of the live oak selected as the dining site.

"More coming after these," Francesco warned, and stopped to wipe his brow with a bandana he pulled from his back pocket.

Margaret marveled at how their relationship had deepened in a smooth, natural curve. Her heart had opened after sharing her wounds and challenges with him, and he in turn had shared his hopes and fears with her. Her new job duties had the unexpected benefit of bringing the two of them together on excursions, she as wait staff and he as driver. They attended prayer services together at the orphanage chapel whenever possible, and even managed to attend Mass together one Sunday when the day's work outing was scheduled for evening.

Margaret was delighted that their dream had taken root and blossomed. The more she learned of him, the more connected she felt. His love for his family and his homeland's traditions resonated with her, and their shared regret at being so far from loved ones drew them closer together. Francesco had told her that, like her, he felt at home in the warm family atmosphere at the orphanage, where everyone had welcomed him with open arms.

Two fellow staff members hurried over and started helping Francesco unload tables and chairs. They set them atop quilts and blankets Margaret had arranged on the sandy mixture of grass and leaves under the tree.

Margaret started unpacking the silverware. Real silver, for a picnic. This wasn't any kind of picnic she'd ever known. This one had all the comforts of a manor house like the one in which she'd once served during a weekend party back in Ireland. She pulled wrapped china plates from a basket with a firm but careful hand. More than four weeks into her new assignment, and she hadn't so much as chipped a dish. Yes, the sun shone on a new day for her.

Blue Willow dishes? She was so surprised when she unwrapped the protective cloth that the serving platter slipped from her damp hands. It landed with a thud on the blanket.

Margaret inspected the platter to make sure no hairline cracks or other nicks had formed. Gently, she placed the blue and white plate back down in its carton, and released an audible sigh.

"And the record still stands?" asked Francesco, who had walked over to where she sat with head bent over the platter.

"Yes, and it's been over a month now."

"I knew you could do it." Francesco gave her shoulders a quick squeeze before tackling more unloading.

Margaret's momentary discomfort over the platter had been real. She was still on a thin thread with the housekeeper, on a job that was doubly meaningful.

Margaret overlooked the physical demands of the work. She swallowed resentment when guests tossed away half-eaten meals while her family back home scrounged for food. She felt good each time she mailed earnings home, meager though the coins were.

She appreciated how she got to spend more time with Francesco now. He was usually one of the drivers assigned to excursions that included outdoor meal service. His presence brightened her job.

Bridget had even commented that Margaret had stopped complaining. She walked to work each morning in a happy mood, rather than just dutifully grateful for the job. Happy.

Over the weeks, she'd let more of her defenses crumble as she watched Francesco go about his job— kind, cheerful, hard-working, fair. And, saints be praised, in love with her as much as she was with him.

She unpacked more china. This was the first time she'd seen Blue Willow ware used outside the dining room. Even inside, it was reserved for special occasions.

Extra staff had even been assigned to this meal, Margaret had noticed.

Francesco lingered after unloading the last box. He looked back at the wagon. "I better move that far out of the way so it doesn't disturb the view during the meal. What's the big deal about today's picnic? Do you know?"

Margaret shook her head as she snapped out the linen napkins and smoothed their wrinkles before re-rolling the silver in them. "Somebody important is visiting, but that's all I know."

She looked where some of the hotel guests had gathered at the edge of the shimmering lake. She longed to wade in and cool off. That would be a firing offense. It would also mean seeing a mirror image of her hair, which she was certain was in a tangle of frizzed curls from the humidity. Even the aloe gel was no match for the weather.

Margaret snuck a peek at herself in the reflection of a silver water pitcher before she filled it with drinking water from the stone crock Francesco had lugged over.

That was a mistake. She filled the pitcher, poured a few drops of water into her hands, tamped down her tresses and repositioned her waitress cap. That would have to do.

She turned to open another hamper and saw Francesco watching her. He didn't say anything. He didn't have to. His eyes conveyed love, and Margaret's heart responded in kind. Her lips curved upward and his did too. Margaret blew him a kiss. He stepped back in make-believe surprise at the impact of her imaginary caress. He put his hand up to feel where the kiss landed on his cheek and rubbed.

"*Bellissimo!*" he said, with his hand now over his heart. She giggled, stood up, and gave him a slight curtsy.

"Hurry up over there!" called one of their colleagues in a loud whisper. "They're expecting to eat in fifteen minutes."

Margaret and Francesco halted their antics but Margaret still felt a delicious glow as she increased her pace. She arranged china and straightened napkins on the tables, which a colleague had draped in linens.

"Here are the flowers," Francesco said, and gave her a tin pail filled with cut azaleas, early roses, late camellias, fronds of longleaf fern, and sprigs of blooming citrus. She lifted the stems from the water, sorted and organized them, and transferred the bouquets into crystal vases, another luxurious touch to the day. She set the vases in the centers of the tables.

"The roses smell wonderful," she said, and inhaled the fruity spiced scent of the rose-red flowers. "And these orange blossoms. So sweet. I would love to carry both on our wedding day."

"Any flowers you want," Francesco said, and flopped down for a five-minute rest. He leaned his head against the tree trunk. "Did I tell you I wrote my family in Italy about us?"

"You did?!"

"Yes, I wasn't going to keep such good news to myself. I want them to get to know you and love you."

She looked down briefly before meeting his gaze. "I wrote my family about you too," she said. "My mother replied that she'd rather I go with a nice Irish fellow, but since you are Catholic she supposes you are all right." Margaret laughed. "That's high praise from my mama. You should feel honored."

His eyes lit up. "I do. My mother will also be happy for me, for us. It takes a while for letters to travel to my family and back, but I hope to hear from them before too long."

Movement down by the water's edge caught their attention. Rowboats filled with tourists were pulling in to shore, and the visitors already mingling there started to rise and gather their walking sticks and parasols.

Francesco made haste to move the wagon and soon disappeared from Margaret's view. She made final tweaks to the lunch setup. She kept sneaking quick looks to see if Francesco reappeared in the distance. Finally, she saw a glimpse of him so far beyond the picnic grounds she had to squint to make him out. She was happy just knowing he was out there.

An hour later, she almost wished he were back. Then was glad he wasn't. For even his good humor would vanish. The last thing she wanted was Francesco getting in trouble with high-ranking guests because he felt compelled to protect her. She could take care of herself.

She gritted her teeth to keep from back talking to the guests. The indignities that sometimes came with the job were a sore spot for her, one she tried to ignore.

The distinguished guest had turned out to be a titled British man. His boorishness was emphasized by the good manners of the rest of his entourage.

The man treated her and the other workers like they were less than human. He demanded, insulted, and gave ridiculous orders. She forced her mouth to stay closed when he ordered her to hand him a salt shaker when she was at the end of the table and he was inches from the condiment.

She kept her eyes lowered as she walked around to where he sat. Not out of modesty, but so he couldn't see her seethe. When she reached him and leaned to get the salt, he inched close enough to brush the side of her body.

She straightened. "The salt, sir," she said, and handed it to him.

He leered at her and pawed her hand longer and harder than necessary as he grabbed for the shaker.

"I say," he commented to the man next to him, without taking his eyes off Margaret or his hand off hers, "don't you think the maids should undress in this miserable heat? They'd be able to move faster, and they could serve us better. What do you say, lass? Can I assist?" He laughed, as though he'd been clever.

Margaret yanked her hand from his and stepped back. Her breath came in short spurts. Titled or not, he deserved to feel the lash of her tongue. If only.

The man's friend changed the subject. A few of the ladies at the table tittered. Others pretended nothing rude had been said.

The afternoon couldn't end quickly enough for Margaret. "Dear Jesus, help me keep my tongue," she prayed over and over. She swallowed bile when she remembered family lore about British landlords overcharging her Irish ancestors for rent and anything else a body needed to just stay alive.

She distracted herself by ignoring the titled man. Just let him call her again!

Instead, she concentrated on listening to the ladies chatter as she moved around them to pick up leftovers and serve tea and lemon cookies.

"And I was shocked, I tell you, shocked that the woman brought her infant with her," one of the ladies said.

"That's what you get for hiring one of these local nobodies," her friend replied. "What were you thinking?"

The first speaker sniffed. "I was told she's a long-term visitor from a good family in Boston, and I assure you, her Italian is fluent. I need the practice. I don't want to fall behind in my lessons just because I'm vacationing here. We'll be heading for the Continent soon. Still, I wonder, how can the woman be so brazen? I didn't even tell you the worst."

The speaker lowered her voice and her friend leaned toward her. Margaret moved in too. She brushed imaginary crumbs from the tablecloth so she could linger and listen.

"She wears no wedding ring, and her calling card says Miss not Mrs.," the first speaker continued. "You can imagine my dismay. Such low-class behavior."

Her companion laughed. "No ring? But, of course, that explains it. That's why she's here, then. She must be in hiding from polite society. Oh, this is too delicious. Wait until we tell the others. What is the family name? Surely she's not sullying the family reputation by using her real identity on her calling cards. Oh, delightful."

Margaret jumped as the titled man bellowed at her from another section of the table. She moved out of earshot and tried to ignore him. He yelled for her again. Heads began to turn her way. Another staff member rushed over to him but he shook his head and pointed to Margaret. She had to go over to him. She was the help.

"Remove these," he said to her, and waved a hand over the empty dishes in front of him. The edge of one almost touched his rotund stomach. She reached to grab the plate but he put his arm around her back and patted her hip. She sidestepped, but his hold tightened.

She felt her face flush as memories she'd shoved away roared back. She gathered as many pieces of china as possible. Drop them she wouldn't. She channeled her fury and dismay into her grip.

"Excuse me, sir," she said through gritted teeth. She stuck out an elbow and made the movement appear part of a normal table-clearing action. She wanted to dump the remaining half-pitcher of lemonade on him. It tipped by accident and a few drops splattered the tablecloth.

"Worthless help," he barked. "Be off with you." He slapped her derriere. "Go!"

Margaret fled, her breath caught in a choke of shock and disgust. The worst part was that she knew she couldn't report him. She had to pretend it hadn't happened. A complaint from a servant would be her word against his. She didn't stand a chance of being believed, and in fact might be blamed. Like last time.

The past flooded back in a rush. She could almost feel the blood making her head pound. No one ever believed a servant. Her former employer certainly hadn't.

Fury built with ever step. She needed to talk to Francesco. There had to be another way to survive. Had to be! They had to move up their plans to make and sell their handicrafts, for him to open a blacksmith shop, for her to find another job.

Margaret was never so glad to be nearing the end of a shift. She made haste to pack used dishes and leftover food, and channeled her anger and frustration into rapid work. The guests drifted back to the water's edge and to hammocks, which staff members had strung between tree limbs.

The two gossiping ladies were still talking about the woman with the infant when they passed Margaret on their way toward the water. She wondered who they were talking about and made a mental note to ask Bridget.

A thought struck her so forcefully she stopped mid-step, out of sight behind a tree. The woman, the one with the infant, might need a nanny. She, Margaret, was better at tending babies than serving meals. And babies didn't pat one's private areas.

Such inspiration had to come from heaven above, she thought. She couldn't wait to share it with Francesco and Bridget. And hopefully act upon it.

A second thought sobered her enthusiasm. A nanny job would take her away from Francesco. But only during work hours, she told herself. They were building a future together. The steps wouldn't all go in a straight line. They'd manage, she and Francesco.

Margaret shooed away a fly. Stop with the dreaming fancifulness, she told herself. You don't even know who the woman with the baby is, or if a job is available. Yet here you are mooning over hours lost from your love.

The titled guest let out a bray of laughter in the near distance. Margaret grimaced. She saw him sip from a flask, which he then put back into his pocket. He saw her watching him. He started to take a step toward her, but a companion put a hand on his arm and distracted his attention.

Margaret shuddered. Her potential sacrifice of separation from Francesco would be a burden to bear. It was nothing compared to the sacrifice our Lord had made. She blessed herself and felt more at peace as she completed her tasks.

- - -

Margaret spilled out the story on the ride back to the hotel with Francesco. She punctuated her recitation with animated hand gestures. Still wrapped in agitation, she neglected to see his hands tighten on the reins as she revealed the incident's details. She barreled on, telling him about the titled guest and then explaining what happened in the past.

"There's more, Francesco," she said.

"Enough, we go right now to the management," he said. "What else did he do? This I will not stand for."

"No, no, we can't report him and you know it," she protested. "And nothing else happened here."

His grip tightened even more. Then he released and flexed his hands, one at a time. "The dark side to the American dream," he muttered. "I know it's there. I try not to let it bother me. But sometimes it does."

She placed her hand over one of his. "Let it go, Francesco. The way I'm letting go what happened in the past. I didn't tell you what led me to get tangled with the man who stole my crochet money. I had lost my job and with it lost my references. If you don't have good recommendations you can't get another job in a private home in New York City."

"No references? I think I can guess what happened," he said. His voice was grim.

"The lady of the house didn't believe what she saw with her own eyes," Margaret explained. "She blamed me. Her husband had blocked my way out of the library, where I had been dusting. He put his hands on my shoulders, pushed me against the fireplace, and tried to kiss me. His wife walked in and screamed. The husband said I'd thrown myself at him! The wife fired me. Ordered me out, that instant."

Margaret took off her cap and shook her hair free. "I told the truth and told the woman the least she could do was give me a recommendation."

"Which I bet she didn't do," Francesco said.

"She laughed at me. As I stood on the doorstep of that house, with my few belongings, I vowed to find another way to earn a living. That led me to trust that man about the crochet business."

"And that led you here, for which I'm eternally grateful," Francesco finished for her. A hint of his cheer returned.

"Yes, I just wish it hadn't been such a hard journey," she said, her temper and ire dissipating. "But the reward has been good." She gave him a shy smile. "Right now I'm glad you're driving this wagon back instead of the guest barouche. I deserve you more than those guests do."

She shifted to move closer to Francesco on the front bench. He put an arm around her shoulder and pulled her against him.

"The sooner you are out of this job and are my wife, the happier I'll be," he said. "I'll be able to protect you fully from fools and idiots."

"The sooner we both make our own way in life, the better," she added. "In the meantime, I'm going to check about that woman with the baby. Maybe I can get a job with her. Even if can't, the hotel job will be over soon. I've heard that some guests stay until mid-April but most leave at the end of March. The staff starts relocating then, so they can get the northern hotel ready. A job as a nanny or companion would be a gift from heaven. Otherwise I have, at most, about a month-and-a-half left to earn my keep here. At least it's a job."

She leaned on Francesco and relaxed, finally. Exhaustion started to creep in. She closed her eyes and fell silent. Three other colleagues, who rode in the wagon bed amid hampers, tables, and soiled linen, dozed as the wagon rocked along.

"I'll drive you to the orphanage in the cart after work," Francesco said as the hotel came into view. "I should finish grooming the horses and cleaning the wagon about the same time you finish kitchen cleanup."

"Don't rush. I can walk."

"I know, but you've had a rough day and it's the little I can do to help right now. I want to be sure you're home safely."

He looked at her, and in his glance she saw protectiveness mixed with love. It washed over her with warmth. "I'll come find you when I'm done." All would be all right, somehow, someway, in the end.

Afternoon shadows softened the day's brightness and heat, and a breeze floated with a gentle caress. It carried mingled scents of sunbaked pine and sweet orange blossoms, and left her upbeat about possibilities for a bright future.

Chapter 10

A few hours later, after they had washed the dinner dishes, Margaret sipped tea and ate cookies with Bridget in the orphanage kitchen. Through the window, she watched Francesco use the lingering dusk to show the children how to play the game bocce. He'd already introduced half the staff at the hotel to it.

She studied him, and his ease and patience with the young ones, and imagined what a good father he would be. She wondered who their future children would resemble. Would they inherit her feisty attitude and flyaway tresses, or his steady core and thick, dark hair? She loved his embrace of family and his willingness to accept new ways while holding fast to older traditions. They were so alike in that way.

Margaret tore her gaze away. "So, you really think it's a possibility, the nanny job?" Margaret asked Bridget. "I can't believe that woman stayed here the whole time she was with child."

"The entire time," Bridget said. "Afterward, her family made a rather large donation, as they termed it, even after I said there was no obligation. Penelope had been a woman in dire need, without the right kind of family support when she arrived here."

Margaret leaned forward. "What happened? Did she say?"

Bridget's eyebrows arched and her smile faded. "If Penelope chooses to divulge her story to you, that's her choice. You won't be hearing gossip from me."

"Okay, okay." Margaret slunk a bit in her chair. "But you think she'd hire a nurse or companion?"

"Indeed, I think it'd be a perfect solution for her current situation," Bridget said. "I believe she'll be interested. She's a practical, forward-thinking woman. But this carting her baby all over town while she gives language lessons is truly not in anyone's interests, in my opinion. I'll call on her and ask her to tea, and introduce the two of you."

"Better make it evening, just in case," Margaret said. "I can't always get out of the hotel by teatime, even with my new duties."

A shout drew both their attentions toward the open window. Children on the winning side backslapped one another and lauded their victory. Their opponents signaled their intent to even the score with another game, immediately. The two groups circled Francesco and each tried to tug him their way. He laughed, joy spread across his face, and sprinted to the far side of the playing field with children in close pursuit.

- - -

Days and then weeks passed in a rapid succession of hunt breakfasts, picnic lunches, and boating and tennis parties. The spring weather dropped midday hints of the hot summer to come. Margaret felt both anxiety and relief each time she saw another pile of trunks being loaded into a wagon or saw guests, in travel attire, climb into a barouche and wave farewell to friends.

Good riddance, she thought, the day the titled man and his companions departed amid more baggage than she'd seen for any group. "We won't be missing the likes of you," she muttered under her breath, glad she'd been able to sidestep him after the picnic encounter.

She plunked two women's valises atop a massive trunk at the bottom of the outdoor steps. It was a slow morning and she and other wait staff had been directed to help carry light luggage. The regular porters grimaced as they strained to carry large trunks. She saw Hortense staggering down the stairs under a load of hatboxes and a large feather-stuffed coverlet.

"Just ridiculous," she whispered as she passed her friend on the stairs while going up for another load. "I can't believe we were ordered to do this." She remembered Hortense's long-ago comment about how the management didn't hire enough help for the season.

"Almost finished, thank goodness," came Hortense's muffled reply. The coverlet started to slide, and an edge fell out and dragged on the stairs.

"Watch what you're doing there! Don't let that get dirty! Pick it up! Place it straight into the carriage, don't just drop it in the sand!"

The sharp orders came from atop the stairs. Margaret looked up and saw two women in travel suits made of such high quality fabric that she spotted nary a winkle. The women's sleek, glossy tresses were carefully arranged under elegant hats, which irked Margaret. She could feel a frizzy curl stuck to her own damp cheek. It just wasn't fair.

"Here, I've got it," she almost barked out to Hortense, and picked up the dropped edge. They transported the bulky coverlet to the waiting carriage pointed out to them, and positioned it so the occupants would have a cushy ride to the railroad station.

"You have no idea how glad I am to be meeting Miss Penelope Gold today," said Margaret as they finished. "I hope she's my ticket out of here."

"I hope so too," Hortense said. "This is the first time ever that waitresses have been made to move luggage. As if we don't have enough to do, starting to close down this hotel and prepare for the move."

Margaret realized she was going to miss her friend. Friend! She'd actually made a friend here. Hortense had never once judged her brogue or her awkward attempts to mold herself into an American waitress of resort worth. Actually, neither had most of the other staff members. They'd accepted her at arm's length, and after a while seemed to understand she was trying to get through life just like they were. She wondered if she'd been too guarded and vigilant against hurt to notice before now.

She looked at Hortense with new eyes. "I'll write to you this summer, if you like, to let you know how things are going in Persimmon Hollow."

"That would be great," said Hortense. "And I'll fill you in on how Mrs. P is making our lives miserable up north."

"Deal," said Margaret, and they returned to their labors.

Margaret checked the position of the sun more than a few times. Only a couple of hours remained until her meeting with Penelope Gold. She dared to wave at a departing carriage, even though it was against rules and even though Francesco was so focused on his work he didn't turn his head to see her. He'd had to affix two extra horses to drag the weight of people and things. The luggage teetered atop and at the rear of the vehicle.

The emptying hotel meant a gradual and continued lightening of daily tasks for Margaret. She hoped Francesco would be able to get to the orphanage when she met Miss Gold. Just knowing he was nearby would give Margaret a boost of confidence. And he'd learn the outcome of the meeting right away.

The next few hours passed in a rush. No more excursions were planned, and Margaret had been put to work in the kitchen for the final days of the season. She chopped and mixed the vegetables for a celery salad, and felt a thrill of victory when the cook allowed her to mix in the dressing without supervision.

You're not so unteachable, are you, she congratulated herself. By shift's end, she was humming. Today, a new beginning, she hoped. Tomorrow, a life united with Francesco's. Life was finally going her way.

Chapter 11

Excitement drummed in Margaret. She made her way out the servants' entrance and started for home. Home! She even thought of the orphanage as home now. When had that happened? Only Francesco's absence tugged at her. The train must have been late, she guessed. He was probably still out at the station, where he had to stay until all guests and their paraphernalia were aboard the train.

Margaret was just about to cross the railroad tracks when she noticed movement to her side. Francesco headed her way from the stables. She lifted her hand, but lowered it. Her cry of hello dried on her lips as Francesco moved toward her like an old man weighed by years of care. His shoulders bowed and his steps were slow.

"Francesco, what's wrong?" She rushed out to meet him. She reached him and took both his hands in her own.

He met her gaze with a look of pure misery. A blanket of dread fell atop Margaret.

"Are you ill? Hurt? Has someone died? Mother of God, help us! Francesco, what is it?" He watched her with a look that shifted into something impenetrable. He let go of her hands and pulled a crumpled letter from his pocket. That alone alarmed Margaret. Francesco was a man of order and neatness. Crumpled anything usually irked him.

"I didn't open this until I was at the station, waiting for the train," he said. He didn't meet her eyes.

She took the envelope and pulled out the thin paper with hands that had started to tremble. She looked at the slanted handwriting.

"Francesco, I can't read this, it's in Italian!" She thrust it back at him. "Please, tell me what it says. What's happened?"

He glanced up at the sky, appeared to be steeling himself, and looked back at the letter.

She strained to lean in and wanted to hug him but his every movement, his stance, his expression all erected a steely barrier between them. One that hadn't ever been there, not from the first day they met. His gaze spoke misery, mixed with love and hurt.

He swallowed, licked his lips, started to speak, but then closed his mouth and then closed his eyes as he sucked in a deep breath.

The long seconds tortured Margaret. "Are you ill?" she asked.

"No."

"Did you lose your job?"

"No."

"Did someone die?!"

He half turned away before he spoke. "Yes, I'm afraid we did," he said.

"What do you mean?" she demanded. Her dread turned icy. "Francesco, I love you but I can't play a guessing game. I have to get home right away. I have an appointment to meet Penelope Gold. If I'm late, I'll never get a job with her."

"I mean this," he said. He held up the letter that he gripped in his hand. "I mean this letter from my family, their reply to my letter about us."

Ah. His family disapproved.

"Oh, Francesco, no, don't despair, if your family doesn't like the idea right now," she said. "We'll make it work." But the knot of anxiety grew in her.

"We can overcome resistance or disapproval," she insisted. "Love and understanding and time will work. It might take a while. But we can do this."

She had to believe that. Had to.

He shook his head, and for the first time looked fully at her. Sadness shadowed the love in his eyes. "No, you don't understand," he said.

She stared at him.

He inhaled. "We can't get married. Ever."

Margaret took a step back. Of all the imagined scenarios that had raced through her mind in the past minutes, that hadn't been one of them.

"Why not?" Had she been wrong about him all along? Oh, dear God, had she been a fool yet again?

"Because I'm already married."

Chapter 12

He spat out the words, rough and sharp. "I'm already married."

If a heart could drop in a body, Margaret's did. She took another step back, and tried to keep a grip on her emotions. She wanted to scream. Badly.

"How can that be?" She forced herself to keep her words even. Find out more, she told herself. Something is horribly wrong. He's not like everybody else. He's not!

But a tiny voice started to tell her that maybe he was.

Francesco ran a hand through his hair. Margaret noticed he wasn't even wearing his usual cap.

"I'm married because my mother wed me by proxy to some girl she had a matchmaker pick out."

The world narrowed around Margaret. Mockingbird calls sounded impossibly loud. The white-beige of the sand, the green of the trees became stark. She couldn't have heard him correctly.

"This happens all the time in Italy," he continued. "I just didn't think it would happen to me."

He looked defeated, uncertain, sad, and angry all at once.

"Is that even legal?" she asked, unease and disillusionment bubbling from her. "Does the Church allow it? Or is your mother so opposed to you tainting yourself with an Irish girl that she grabbed at any obstacle?"

Margaret couldn't keep the bitterness from her tone. Nor did she want to.

"No!" Francesco reached for her, then put his arms down when she retreated from him.

"No, Margaret, it happened before they even got my letter about you. It takes months for a matchmaker to pair a couple, then for the families to haggle over the details of the marriage settlement. The two people being pushed together usually have nothing to say about the arrangements. But they usually already have eyes for each other. This is just odd."

Margaret stared. Odd, indeed. Was it even true, as he claimed, that he knew nothing about it? Francesco started to become a stranger before her eyes.

"Usually, the girl or guy has already signaled their interest in a particular person," Francesco went on, his words rapid, his eyes beseeching hers. "They indicate by a word to a parent, or a glance after church or—" He stopped and shoved his hands in his pockets. "It's complicated and mixed up in Italian culture. It's, well, you don't want to hear all this, all the details."

"You're right. I don't." An iron vise and stab of pain melted into a hardness in Margaret.

"There isn't anyone else, I swear on a Bible, I didn't leave a sweetheart in Italy," Francesco said. "I can't figure how this happened. The local girls bat their lashes at my brothers, not me."

He did appear perplexed. Or maybe he was just a good actor.

Anger kept her tears at bay. "Like I already asked, and you didn't answer: A marriage by proxy, is that even real?"

"In my hometown it always is. My, uh, bride is being put on the boat for America in a month, or at least that's what my mother writes."

For the first time since the nightmare of a conversation began, Francesco's grip on his temper appeared to waver. He picked up pinecones scattered on the ground around them, and pitched them hard into the woods, one after another.

Meanwhile, Margaret's heart crumbled. She had to leave, yet couldn't make her feet move.

"I don't even have a house to put a wife in," Francesco said, almost to himself. "And when I do, I dreamed of you in it."

"Can't you get out of this mess?" She grasped, like a drowning woman, at anything she could think of.

He shook his head. "I don't see how. It's too late. Plus my entire family would lose face. That would be a big deal, and unthinkable, in the small town I come from. For me to back out would show incredible dishonor to my parents. I can't shame them in such a way."

"But you're in America now. I'm in America. We're both in a new world that you, especially, have been excited about." Her words trailed off, and he didn't answer.

Margaret closed her eyes. How could they be wrenched apart by some stupid tradition thousands of miles away? How could he not stop it?

"I've already written back, questioning the whole deal," Francesco said. "I was so surprised I borrowed paper, an envelope, and postage from one of the guests in my carriage while we waited at the station. I don't care if I get in trouble for it. I scribbled out my protest and my questions and sent it out with the mail just now on the train."

"I guess that's a start," she said. But her words felt hollow and feeble. She wasn't even sure she believed him. Even if he did send the letter, weeks, maybe months, could pass before a reply arrived.

"I have to tell you, Margaret, I'm not hopeful," Francesco said. "I can't lie and say we should keep our hopes up."

The misery of his expression echoed her own. A sad silence settled over them. Margaret's dismay faded as anger seeped in every crevice.

"Well, then, that's it, right?" she blurted out. "We just say goodbye? Fine. I'll be off, then. I have to get to my meeting."

She turned on her heel, leaving a deep impression in the sand, and started to stalk off. Tears pooled. Margaret blinked them away. She, Margaret Murphy, would not shed one watery drop in front of the lying man who had just broken her heart. Not one. No. He and his entire country could fall off the map and she wouldn't care a whit.

"Margaret!" She heard the note of desperation at the edge of the voice.

She walked faster.

"Margaret!" he called, but he didn't move to come after her.

She strode away as fast as she could with any dignity, until finally, blessedly, he stopped calling her name. And then she let the tears fall.

Chapter 13

Margaret stood outside the orphanage door. She gulped deep breaths and willed her nerves to quiet down. No one got a job by stepping into an interview all flustered and shaky.

Oh, but she ached.

"St. Jude, please help this impossible cause— me," she murmured. She stood rigid in front of the door, with eyes closed and hands gripped into fists by her sides. "Take my woes to our Lord through as many prayers as you can send my way. Blessed Mother, I beseech you, please ask your Son to help me. Amen."

She blessed herself and stood in silent prayer until her heaving lessened. The Lord had borne a cross far heavier than anything she'd had to bear, she knew. She remembered her mother reminding her and her siblings of that when childhood mishaps had loomed large in their small worlds.

Margaret prayed a calming Hail Mary. She repeated the prayer until a modicum of peace rested on her shoulders. Squaring them, she put her hand on the door latch and went inside.

Bridget and Penelope Gold rose from the anteroom bench as she entered. Penelope studied her, while Bridget's expression of concern radiated from her eyes and face.

"There you are, Margaret," Bridget said. "Only twenty minutes late." The unspoken reprimand dripped through the words. "I was just telling Miss Gold you must have been detained at work. Yes?"

Margaret looked from one to the other. She could either lie or tell the truth. Her earlier deception at work to attend Mass was a heavy memory. She didn't like being saddled by untruths. They nagged at her conscience.

"Begging your pardon, Miss Gold, Bridget," she said, and dipped a small curtsy toward Penelope and a nod to her cousin. She straightened and lifted her gaze. "I was detained, yes. Only it was by the news that the man I thought was my future husband is already married by proxy to a woman of his family's choosing in Italy."

Saying it aloud made it even more real. Bridget's eyes widened and Penelope's narrowed.

"Indeed," Penelope said. She assessed Margaret but didn't say anything else.

"My goodness, we'll hash that out over tea, later, Margaret," said Bridget, with emphasis on the word later. With brisk steps, she ushered them all to the side table by the window.

Someone had set out glasses of lemonade. Sweat had already coated their perimeters. Wet rings pooled around the glass bottoms on the crocheted table runner.

"Please, sit here, Penelope," Bridget said, all business again. "Thank you for meeting with my cousin today. I pray you will find her accommodating."

They sat down in silence. In a quick glance, Margaret took in Miss Gold's fashionable dress and smooth chignon. The lady sat with quiet confidence. What she would give to be so put together all the time. But where was the baby? The hotel guests had gossiped about how Miss Gold toted the child everywhere.

Bridget's glance told Margaret to get on with things. At the same time, Penelope initiated the interview.

"You wished to speak to me about a job?" Penelope prodded.

Margaret inhaled and dove in.

"Yes, thank you so much for your time, Miss Gold," Margaret began in her best professional manner, and then didn't stop talking. "I apologize for my tardiness. The approaching end of my seasonal job at the railroad's hotel led me to inquire about employment as a nanny, or perhaps as a companion for you, miss, or a maid, whatever you might need."

She sipped a breath and made an effort to slow down her words. "I am trained and willing to apply myself to all those tasks or any others, and would be very honored to work for you." She looked down and fiddled with the table runner, and neatened the edge closest to her.

She glanced up at Penelope. "With today's shock, you can see my future is open," she added. "I have every reason to hope you will find favor with me." She looked around. "But where is the babe?"

Uh, oh, job lost before it was even offered. Margaret felt her cheeks flame for asking such an impertinent question. Bridget glanced upward as though seeking help from above.

Penelope smiled for the first time. "She's with Sister Rose, who took her upstairs so the children could see her. Many of them remember me from my stay here."

"I helped my mama with the little ones," Margaret said. "I'm the oldest, so I learned from the start. I've also been out to service, so I know maid and companion duties. At the hotel, I learned the proper way to set a table and wait on guests, and I've even learned how to make some fancy summer dishes in the kitchen."

"Your cousin gives you a glowing recommendation," Penelope said. "I know the value of her word. If I hire you, what will happen if your young man comes around and says he's free and wishes to marry?"

Margaret closed and opened her mouth. She wanted to say, "That will never happen," but different words spilled out.

"I won't lie and say I don't wish it were so, miss," Margaret said, and tried to smile to cover her nervousness. "Even if the arranged marriage weren't in the way, he isn't free to wed for several months because of prior commitments about work. I too am committed to helping my family. And we both wish, I mean we would wish if it happened, to work long enough to start life without debt and with the ability to continue helping our families."

Her voice trailed off. Don't be telling the lady your life story just because she seems nice, she told herself. Miss Gold was obviously a woman of quality. She was soft-spoken but assured, and carried herself with a quiet poise that implied she knew where she stood in life and expected that everyone else did too. Despite her confidence, she didn't put on the airs Margaret saw in some of the hotel guests.

Poised or not, the lady wanted to hear correct, servant-like answers, Margaret was sure. Not her continued blabbering and familiarity.

"In such an event, you would continue to work for me until other suitable arrangements could be made?" Penelope asked. "Until an acceptable replacement was found?"

Margaret stared at her a moment, her eyes wide. Miss Gold must have had some bad servant experiences. "Oh, yes, miss, absolutely! I would never just run off, for any reason!"

"I like your directness, Margaret," said Penelope, using her first name for the first time, which Margaret interpreted as a good sign.

"Actually, you remind me of my former lady's maid," Penelope added.

Oh. Competition. Margaret pressed her hands together on her lap. Please let that other girl be somewhere far away, never to return.

"Since I assume you and everyone else within a hundred miles knows of my, uh, circumstances, I don't mind admitting that I lost that maid overnight for reasons no one in my family would discuss with me," Penelope explained.

"Only later, did I put two and two together and realize she had gotten herself in the family way without benefit of a husband. I never learned the particulars, for she was dismissed without my immediate knowledge. I undertook a thorough search for her that continued even after I relocated here. The detective I hired found evidence she returned to Ireland. Where, I don't know."

Margaret was delighted.

"I have the resources to deal with situations," Penelope said. "She did not. I regret I wasn't able to be of assistance to her. However, I continue the search, so I can help support her should she be found and be in need."

"You are a saint," Margaret blurted out. How very kind of her, to do such for a servant.

"Hardly," said Penelope, and her lips twitched with some inner knowledge. "When does your hotel job end?"

"Week after next," Margaret said.

"Would you consider living in-residence with me and taking a job as a dual companion and nurse?" Penelope asked.

"I'd be honored!" Margaret almost couldn't believe her luck. "But, uh, may I ask a question?"

"As I said, I liked your directness. You are free to speak to me at will."

"Will I be able to come here and help my cousin by teaching the children how to crochet, and will I be able to attend Mass at my church?"

"Of course, to both. We will attend Mass together. Your church will soon be my church too," Penelope said.

"Honestly? Saints be praised!"

"Margaret." Bridget shook her head in warning.

"It's all right," Penelope said. "Yes, I'm taking Catechism lessons, Margaret. And I visit here fairly often, myself. I'm a bit surprised we haven't crossed paths yet."

"Until just recently, the hotel kept me busy most daylight hours and into the night, Miss Gold."

"Penelope."

"Miss Penelope."

Penelope Gold looked at a delicate watch affixed to a tiny chain at her waist. She rose. "I'm due to give a language lesson in town shortly. Rose should be bringing Grace back any moment."

As if on cue, the sound of footsteps and the chatter of children sounded in the far end of the hallway. Sister Rose entered first, carrying a plump, grinning baby girl who reached with her arms the second her eyes latched onto her mother.

Penelope rose and took her baby, Margaret close on her heels.

"Say hello to Miss Margaret, your new nurse," Penelope cooed to the baby.

"Hello, little one. Such a sweet little babe you are." Margaret felt an immediate and fierce protectiveness toward Grace, who stared at her, round-eyed, and then smiled.

"May I hold her?" Margaret asked.

Penelope transferred Grace to Margaret's arms and then watched as the baby tugged on Margaret's cap, caused it to tip down to one side, and reached for the curls that sprang loose. Margaret laughed aloud for the first time since Francesco's awful news had darkened her world. She kissed Grace atop her head and cradled her.

"Then, everything is settled?" Bridget interjected.

"Yes," Penelope said. "And I really do have to leave now."

Margaret handed back the baby and reached to fix her cap.

"I'll expect you at my residence week after next," Penelope said. "And let your hair be its normal self. No need to force it under such a cap. Grace will just keep pulling it off, anyway."

As the door closed behind Penelope, Margaret sank down in bliss, then shot up from the chair.

"What?!" Bridget asked.

Margaret yanked open the door and ran out after Penelope. "Miss Gold! Miss Gold."

Penelope turned and waited.

"I forgot to ask." Margaret came to a short halt. "We didn't discuss, uh, Miss Gold, what will my pay be?"

"Oh, dear, see how much I need help? To forget such a part of the discussion." She pondered for a few minutes. "Will three dollars and fifty cents per week, no, make it four dollars per week, suffice? Plus your room and board, of course."

Margaret stared at her. "May the Lord grant your every wish, now and forever, Miss Gold," she said.

"Thank you, thank you, thank you. It's more than I could have dreamed of."

Her dream of life with Francesco may have been shattered, but the Lord had answered her prayers for a future caring for Miss Gold's baby.

Chapter 14

A month later, Margaret struggled to adjust to her new circumstances in the ever-growing heat of almost-summer Florida. She liked her job. But everything was so different. And depressing without Francesco. Without Bridget. Without the orphans or even the other workers at the hotel.

Lord, how she missed being around a lot of people.

She wandered around Penelope's quiet house while mother and baby were on a private visit. She trailed her hand over a tabletop. All the house's furnishings were neat, and the décor had just the right touch of class. Not too fussy and not too severe. Margaret even had her own room. Penelope was a true lady and baby Grace was a joy, a sweet, quiet baby. It was the easiest job Margaret ever had.

So what in Our Lady's name is wrong with you, Miss Margaret Murphy, she wondered as she went into her room and plopped in the chair by the window.

Her wounded heart.

Margaret couldn't stop Francesco's image from rising to the forefront of her mind. She'd avoided him at the hotel and had refused to see him the three times he'd come to the orphanage to see her. He hadn't returned after that. Her hotel job ended a couple of days after his final attempt.

She'd packed her few belongings and accepted Bridget's offer to let one of the older orphans drive her into town in the cart. She'd tried to make Bridget, the other sisters, and all the orphans promise not to tell Francesco where she was going, but none of them would agree.

Well, if he shows up here I'll close the door in his face, she thought. Not that he would. She remembered his reservations about townsfolk and his troubles with unruly characters. He wasn't on steady ground yet in American society. He certainly had no idea of the etiquette of making a social call in town, on a woman who refused to see him.

She reached for her lacework on the dressing table and started to crochet with furious intensity on the half-finished edging for a cradle blanket.

Ten minutes later, Margaret set down her work in her lap and looked out the window. She imagined Francesco strolling up the walkway to the small front porch. He'd smile at her, with a happy look in his eyes and lift in his step. They'd sit together on the small swing. She remembered how right it felt when they just sat together, even without talking or doing some activity. The sun had shone inside her even on rainy days at those times.

She looked down at the slender crochet hook in her hand and at the stilled thread of yarn that draped slackly over it. *It's over, Margaret. Francesco isn't coming.*

He wouldn't, she knew, not even if he found out where she was. Not only was he reluctant to come to town, her own recent behavior had told him clearly to stay away. Penelope's wood-frame house, on a side street off the busier main road, was two miles from the hotel and two million miles from Francesco's heart.

She sighed. How did one will oneself to fall out of love? She really needed to know. She'd been down before, but she always pulled herself up. Was trying to do so right now, in fact, in this job in this house. But her heart wasn't mending.

She yanked on the yarn, and made a few stitches so tight she had to pull them out. Her job left her plenty of time to work on her handicraft, especially now that she had no beau. Before the next tourist season arrived, she'd have enough items to sell in the tourist store the Taylors owned near the hotel's railroad station, just as Francesco and Bridget had urged her to do. She wondered if Francesco was working on andirons and trivets and other ironwork to sell.

Margaret stopped trying to crochet. Melancholy washed over her. She set her work aside and picked up her rosary from the nightstand. She made the Sign of the Cross, said the Apostle's Creed, and rolled the first bead between her fingers. "Our Father," she murmured as she closed her eyes and prayed the rest in silence.

- - -

Margaret felt as droopy as the day's heat, which stifled everything indoors and out without hint of a breeze. Baby Grace was cranky, and even Penelope's normally placid demeanor edged toward impatience.

"No man is worth the amount of moping you're indulging in," Penelope said as they sat on the front porch. "Don't you think it's gone on too long?"

Margaret soothed the baby with puffs of air from a fan woven from palm fronds. "'Tis truth you're speaking, I know."

The day was too hot for talking. Grace finally fell asleep and Margaret set down the fan and opened her workbag. She pulled out her current project, a lace shawl in cream-colored cotton, nearly complete. Being careful to keep her working stitch marked, she opened the shawl to review the flow and tension of the thread.

"Beautiful," Penelope said.

"Came out even better than I expected," Margaret said. "We'll see how it fares in the Taylor store next tourism season. When I met with Mrs. Taylor, she suggested I supply a range of different items so we can see what the tourists prefer."

"Good idea," Penelope said. A few moments later, she sat upright in her chair. "I have an even better one. Please come with me to the dressmaker tomorrow. I have an appointment in the morning to review the newest fabrics. Bring that shawl and a few other examples of your best work."

The next morning, before the sun rose high enough to bake away breathable air, Margaret wheeled the baby carriage and walked the few blocks with Penelope to dressmaker Josefa Gomez's shop.

Discover Josefa Gomez's story in Book 2:
***Stitching A Life in Persimmon Hollow*, which can be read as a stand-alone book.**

"I've heard she's as talented as any fine dressmaker in Paris," Margaret said as they turned the corner and saw the shop's awning.

"She is. Women who patronize her when visiting here continue to send orders to her through the mail year-round. She has a good eye for quality and trends. That's why I want her to see your shawl."

Margaret gulped. She knew her lacework was good, but high-fancy good? She'd dismissed the idea of showing samples to this dressmaker as soon as she noted the quality of Penelope's custom clothing. This dressmaker was out of her league.

"My work isn't up to her standards," she said. She should have flat out refused to go this morning. But Penelope was a gracious employer who made few demands.

"I beg to differ," Penelope said and turned the doorknob and entered the shop. "Let's see what she says."

It was too late to turn back now.

"Ah, good morning!" called out Josefa. "Welcome."

Margaret watched as Josefa, who was younger than she'd expected, rose from her sewing machine, welcomed Penelope, cooed over the baby, and then turned to her with outstretched hands. Penelope made introductions and wasted no time getting to the point.

"Margaret works for me, but she is a talented crochet lace maker who's interested in finding outlets for her products. I asked her to bring some things to show you."

Josefa's eyebrows framed an expression of interest. Her gaze darted to Margaret's workbag. "May I see?"

Margaret hated how her hand trembled as she carefully drew out and unfolded the shawl, two sets of collars and cuffs, and a table runner. She set them atop burgundy fabric Josefa had laid out on the large worktable in the center of the room.

Margaret had to admit, the lacework pieces were pictures of beauty when displayed this way.

"What fine work!" Josefa exclaimed. "Margaret, where have you been hiding?"

"At the railroad's hotel, until just a short time ago when I went to work for Miss Penelope."

"She plans to make and sell items in Agnes and Seth's store," Penelope said. "But I wondered if she could expand her range to include special orders from you, should the need arise among your clients."

"I could sell one of these shawls with almost every custom outfit," Josefa said. She inspected the shawl's even stitches and delicate design. "And collars and cuffs, why, some of my clients have already asked for them. They're always in demand. How soon can you start to provide me with merchandise? I'd like to build up a small stock as well as handle custom orders and designs. And, Margaret, my clients pay nicely for quality."

Margaret wasn't sure she believed her ears. Her dream was taking shape as beautifully as the crocheted rose motif of the shawl. She wanted to run and share the news with Francesco. Couldn't wait to tell him! A pinch stabbed at her heart as soon as the thoughts rushed through her head. She pursed her lips and reminded herself to look toward a future that didn't include Francesco.

"I can start providing merchandise right away," Margaret said. "You can keep the shawl here now. I have to meet my obligations to the Taylors, but the items for the store aren't due until next tourist season. My job allows me time for my crochet. The baby is so good, and Penelope tends to her as much as I do."

As if she'd heard them, Grace awakened and started to fuss. Penelope picked her up and rocked her.

"The Taylors are like family to me," Josefa said. "I'll talk to Agnes and Seth about who gets to claim more of your work." Her eyes sparkled with a hint of mischievousness that made her instantly likeable, and far less formidable, to Margaret.

Josefa draped the shawl around a display mannequin, went to her desk and returned with money in hand for Margaret. "We start our business agreement today," she said, and pressed the bills into Margaret's hand. "Is this enough?"

Margaret glanced at the money, almost gulped aloud, and could do little more than nod agreement. The payment was more than enough. She calculated what she'd be able to send home after investing a portion in more yarn. Thanks be to God, she thought. 'Tis a miracle, to be able to provide such assistance and pay down her debt.

"I'd like to immediately order three more, same pattern but in silk and one each in deep blue, burgundy, and black," Josefa said. "First, please do another in the cream-colored cotton."

"Aye, right away," was all Margaret could croak. Then a grin broke out on her face and she felt her voice come back. "I can't express my thanks enough!"

"Oh, I'm the one who's thankful," Josefa said. "You've just increased the value of my business. Our business partnership will benefit us both."

Penelope looked delighted.

For the first time since her awful breakup with Francesco, Margaret felt hope flood through her. Her crochet business was coming true, in a town she never imagined could grip a hold on her. Funny, how she was coming to appreciate Persimmon Hollow.

"Looks like I may have to start a search for a new nanny and companion," Penelope said, her words light.

"Oh, no, I won't go far. I couldn't bear to leave the little one," Margaret said. And laughed. A true, heartfelt laugh the likes of which she hadn't expressed in weeks.

Chapter 15

Two weeks later, Margaret steeled herself. She'd known she'd have to face Francesco sometime, and that time had come.

No excuse in the world would allow her to skip the big party at the orphanage. The namesake feast days of three children fell within the same week. The orphanage celebrated the occasion with a festive party each year. She'd heard about the event months ahead of time.

She hoped Francesco hadn't been invited, but knew he'd probably be there. Bridget had told her he still coached the youngsters in bocce.

Margaret mentally prepared herself to be cool and indifferent. And then begged Penelope to help her fashion her hair. Penelope went a step further. She insisted that Margaret wear one of her garments—a sprigged linen whose pattern of small green flowers and leaves accented Margaret's hair and eyes.

"I'm just doing this to look good for the party," Margaret said.

"Uh, huh, of course," Penelope said. The baby gurgled.

The summer heat abated and party day was as perfect as could be, ideal for an outdoor get-together of cake, tea and lemonade, and games of croquet and bocce. Margaret scanned the crowd as she, Penelope, and the baby rolled up in Penelope's carriage. She was both relieved and disappointed that she didn't see

Francesco. She wanted him to see her make her entrance like a lady who'd recovered from heartbreak.

Penelope exited the carriage and took the baby from her. "Go, visit with your cousin and the children," she said.

Determined to have a good time, Margaret walked with fixed steps toward the people clustered in the shade of oak trees a short distance beyond the orphanage building. She was just past the end of the building when Francesco stepped out from the side and intercepted her.

She halted and could almost see her smooth exterior fly away.

"Margaret," Francesco said, and took a light hold of her arm. His eyes widened. "You look...you are so beautiful. That dress. Your hair."

She moved to shake free. His words were like barbs, not balms.

He immediately removed his hand.

"I'd like to talk to you," he said with a quiet dignity.

She was in danger of relenting. "What were you doing? Lying in wait for me?" she asked instead.

"Actually, yes."

She couldn't resist a smile, but immediately forced it away.

"I have nothing to say to you, Francesco. That's all in the past."

"I have plenty to say, if you'll just hear me out."

"Stop, Francesco! What can you possibly say that will make anything better? Leave me alone. I'm trying to stop loving you. It's not like you to toy with me."

He was serious and intent. "I'm not toying, Margaret. I've missed you more than you know. I'd like to offer exactly what will make everything better, if you'll allow me to."

She blinked hard. *Find your strength, Margaret. Borrow some of that dignity from your employer and your cousin. Nothing can resolve this situation. It's too late.*

With quiet assurance, she straightened. "You must know I will never deign to be a man's mistress, if that's what you were going to offer," she said. "I'd appreciate if you let me go live my life."

He grinned at her.

How dare he!

"As long as you live it as my wife."

She locked gazes with him. "Have you lost your mind?"

"I even worked up the nerve to go into town to speak with you, to ask you," he said. "You weren't home. Your cousin said you'd be here today, so I forced myself to wait."

She kept a hard gaze on him, but her body tingled. He'd come to town after her. Town, his least favorite place. Something major must have happened.

"Margaret, I got another letter, last week."

All of a sudden, her other Francesco was back—the happy, confident young man ready to mold his future.

"I'm not married!" He almost shouted. He stretched his arms wide as though alerting the entire world.

A bud of cautious hope blossomed in Margaret.

"You wouldn't believe the uproar back home," Francesco said. "What a mess it was! It turns out the bride was expecting to marry my cousin Francesco. He lives with my family, that's why there are two of us with the name." The light in his eyes crackled with happiness.

"Her mother went around lamenting, loudly, that my family had tricked hers, and that no daughter of hers was going to America," Francesco continued.

"On and on it went. I can imagine the drama, the wailing, the arguing. My cousin Francesco was so mad he spent money to send a telegram from where he works, which is hours from my family's town. Insisted he'd never be separated from the woman he loved, that he'd follow her to America if he had to. I'm so glad I wasn't there!"

He paused to take a breath.

"The parish priest had to get involved," Francesco said. "The dowry had to be returned, and the matchmaker yelled at for messing everything up. That's how things went wrong. The matchmaker came to my house to make the marriage arrangements, but she had gotten the Francescos mixed up. See, my cousin and I, neither of us lives in town any longer. We both work far away. That's why there was a proxy marriage. But my cousin is only up the peninsula in Italy, not all the way across the ocean. He returned home in record time."

Margaret, shocked into silence, waited, poised on the edge of joy.

"Margaret!" Francesco shouted her name this time, a look of delight and love on his face, and his hands on her arms. "I'm a free man! Will you marry me?"

He got down on one knee. "Beg my forgiveness. I forgot to kneel!"

Margaret half cried, half laughed, and croaked out a "Yes, yes, yes."

Francesco rose to his feet and pulled her into his arms. He kissed her lips, her eyes, and the hair that framed her face. Her hands were around him and on him. She found his lips again.

She burrowed closer to him. How she had missed him, his warmth, his cheer, and his love. He lifted her off her feet and twirled her around.

The sound of applause, cheering, and shouts of hurrah surrounded them. They broke apart. There, yards from where they embraced, stood every partygoer, enjoying the show.

"They must have guessed," Francesco said.

"Sounds like it," she said.

They started to make their slow way toward the others.

"I can't believe you came to town," she said.

"Your cousin learned the troublemakers weren't residents, and I forced myself to go to town. I kept thinking of your courage in staying here when you didn't want to, in order to help your family. I went and introduced myself to the livery-stable owner. It was a big step for me. He encouraged me to work in the shop during slow periods at the hotel in summer. He even ordered horseshoes."

"I dreamed that you'd come visit me," she said. "I waited and wished. I can't believe I wasn't there. I'm almost always there. Oh! Maybe it was the day we were at the dressmaker shop."

The story of her success at Josefa's shop tumbled out, and her words fell one atop another in her enthusiasm.

"Yes!" Francesco said. "I knew it. I knew you would go big as soon as your work was discovered."

"I'm going to make items for the Taylor store, too, for next tourist season," she said.

"Me, too. I went to speak with Mr. Taylor right after I dropped off the last passengers of the season. I've been spending my time making hooks, candleholders, spider irons, and things like that." He inhaled. "When I wasn't rehearsing what to say when I finally had you in my arms again."

He pulled her into a quick embrace and kiss.

She gripped his hands and smiled up at him.

"Oh, Francesco, look how things are dropping right into place. You, me, the store, the dressmaker, the livery stable."

He nodded yes and hugged her again. "We'll reach our dreams," he said. "We'll conquer all obstacles, pay the debts and bills, and be free to marry."

"And enjoy every step of the way together," she added.

He kissed her hand. They started toward the others again. The road ahead was long. Margaret knew it would be a lengthy engagement. But that didn't matter. They were already traveling together, walking as one, soon to be united forever.

The End

*Most modern biblical translations cite the verse in Chapter 7 as Psalm 143:8. The 142:8 citation used in this book is from the public-domain Douay-Rheims version of the Bible.

About the author

Gerri Bauer's idea of the perfect day always includes a book, preferably one with a happy ending. She is the author of short stories and the Persimmon Hollow Legacy novels. A native of New York City, Gerri lives in Florida with her husband. You can learn more on her webpage, gerribauer.com, which includes links to her short stories (which you can read for free), novels, blog, and social media sites.

Made in the USA
Coppell, TX
28 October 2019

10551336R00081